Global capitalism has fallen on hard times. But for Patrick McCarry, a down-on-his luck Wall Streeter, opportunities beckon along the Danube.

He's helping a folksy Midwestern client pick through failed businesses for a vacant factory.

Maybe the client plans to build small engines.

Or maybe he knows that if he's right on the doorstep of the Balkans, pretty soon somebody is going to want to buy machine guns.

DEATH IN

Budapest

Novels *by* JAMES L. ROSS

Death in Budapest   (2012)
Long Pig   (2011)

DEATH IN

Budapest

JAMES L. ROSS

PERFECT CRIME BOOKS

Printed in the United States of America.
Perfect Crime Books™ is a registered Trademark.
Cover photograph: iStock. Used by permission.

This book is a work of fiction. The places, events and characters described herein are imaginary and are not intended to refer to actual places, institutions, or persons.

Library of Congress Cataloging-in-Publication Data
Ross, James L.
Death in Budapest / James L. Ross.
ISBN: 978-1-935797-17-3

First Edition: February 2012

For Alice A. Hoover

and in memory of Ralph

1

I crawled forward through the snow, pulled a glove off and felt his neck because I couldn't be sure. He had moaned a few minutes ago, as I was wallowing behind trees ten yards away, keeping my face down in case the shooter had more ideas. Now, with my fingers numb, all I could tell was that the flesh on Milo's neck was slippery and hard.

He was curled on his side, faced away from me, snow dusting the oily tweed suit he had worn the last couple of days, no overcoat; a short guy, not really rodent-like but I thought of him that way. I stayed propped on my elbows, looking across his shoulder. Snow was blowing through the wooded cul-de-sac that abutted the government square, rising in spirals under street lamps, swirling toward the pimped-up wedding cake of the neo-Gothic Parliament building. There had to be guards near the building who might want to hear what had happened. I didn't plan to tell them.

"Wind's bad," Milo had complained, turning up the collar of his suit coat. We had walked from the car, out in the open a couple of minutes. "Let's step in here," he said. "My dude will be along."

"In here" was a few yards off the path. The deep U of trees wasn't much of a windbreak. If I was going to wait for a government worker who was willing to be bribed, I would have preferred to wait in a steamy-windowed café where the brandy was cheap. It hadn't occurred to me that I was being careless coming here until Milo's arms flew up, like a double Deutscher Grusse, and the air blew out of his lungs and the impact of the slug knocked him down.

I heard the shot about a second after he grunted. I knew nothing about guns, but I knew that the lag put the shooter pretty far out, maybe a hundred yards, which would be back toward the car park. Pretty decent plinking, through wind and snow, if he had been aiming for one of us. Even better if he got the one he wanted.

"How much of the money did you bring?" Milo had asked.

"All of it." It wasn't much, but I was still thinking in New York terms. If you were bribing someone on Wall Street, ten thousand wasn't much.

"That's good," he said.

Maybe he gave a little sign then to whoever was behind us. What I thought of as not much money would feed his family of eight for a year if they stuck to goulash, and if he had a family of eight.

I gave Milo another look.

He looked dead.

There was no frost hanging from his nose, no breath melting snow.

I got up and put a couple of trees between us. The wind was coming off the river. Nothing lay that way except perhaps a chance to get myself cornered. The natural direction to go was away from the government center, toward the city center. It was pretty along here, snow devils dancing outside the trees, bare black limbs slicked with ice. When I came past a tree and a low stone wall was ahead, I knew that if I had been a shooter waiting to see who came out, this was where I would wait.

And there he was. Hunkered down, head capped with snow, frozen arms wrapped around himself—looking on second glance like an iron trash basket. I hadn't quite shit myself, but it was close. Snow-covered rubbish lay scattered nearby on the path.

The cold had my eyes streaming. I pushed the tears away, straightened my back, and hurried on. There was an avenue not far ahead where I might find a taxi.

If you wanted to kill Milo Sipos, you wouldn't waste a skilled gunman. A tray of rat poison would do. He sold introductions—including introductions to people he had never met. Three hours ago he had introduced me to a basement strip club called Dolce Vita, where he was on familiar ground, insisting I needed to see cultural sights while we worked out the size of the bribe I would have to pay to get what I wanted, which was access to the chief adviser to the finance minister.

Dolce Vita was overheated, with a low, stained ceiling and silver paper on the walls.

We sat down, and Milo complained, "These Serb girls are all diseased," and spat on the floor, betting that management wouldn't throw us out when he had an American with a credit card in tow. He told me more. "The girls cross the border, too many of them, Gypsies, Albanians, East Germans, Romanians. You name it. You would be amazed."

A girl tried to approach us for a drink. Milo flapped his hand, which held a lighted cigarette between the third and fourth fingers, and she withdrew.

He hadn't shaved. The collar of his denim shirt was shiny with grime. He wore a necktie with large sliced burgundy dots and a tweedy suit that hadn't fit any better the day before.

He told me that personally he was doing fine, which was a lie. Nobody was doing fine. The global capitalist machine had sprung half its gears and was bucketing downhill. It was true in New York. It was true in Budapest. Nobody was sure there wasn't a series of cliffs ahead.

"The big drag is the refugees," Milo said.

He touched the cigarette to his lips, showing me raw knuckles. A girl on stage was laughing loudly at something as she moved lethargically. The stage was surrounded on three sides by chrome monkey bars. Pink satin had curled up from serrated water stains at the edges of the platform, which rattled each time her foot touched it. As far as I could tell from signs on the street, Budapest had more "szex" clubs like Dolce Vita than it had pastry shops.

I checked my watch. Either I could buy my way to Tamás Gabor, who was the man I needed, or I couldn't.

Milo said, "There's more money in women than anything else. A lot of supply, but the demand is there. You were in Vienna?"

"No."

"They bring the girls by buses down from the Czech Republic, drop them off on the Stubenring for a couple of days. The girls tell the cops, 'Oh, sir, I'm looking for work in the cabarets.' They're looking for bank clerks who want to be serviced at lunchtime. It is very low-end business."

I wondered if he was trying to sell me a string of prostitutes.

"Investment banking," Milo said. "That's the way to make money, isn't it?"

"It used to be. So when do I talk to Gabor?"

"Soon, I hope." He settled back, breaking eye contact with me so he could watch a girl who climbed the monkey bars dressed in a red satin hat, black boots, sagging white skin. "This one—she's no Serb. This one could be from Germany. Clean as a whistle, I'll bet."

So he was pimping for the place, which explained why they let him spit on the floor.

I said, "How well do you know really know Tamás Gabor?"

He looked away. "I know his person at the Ministry. That is enough to get you in. I'm sad that we have to pay the thief." A little helpless gesture. "But we have to live in the world we're given, eh?"

That meant that he wanted to drink at my expense, tickle information out of me, and hope he could find a deal on the side. So he pretended to like the idea of capitalism washing the winter streets like warm spring rain, soaking everything and turning it green. Fifteen years ago, when I was getting my M.B.A., that had been true. None of us had expected a new ice age.

"I think ten thousand would be about right," he said.

"For Gabor's man or one of the whores?"

"Heh. Have another whiskey. It's my turn to buy."

He would pick me up outside my hotel once I had the money. "Meet me on the cross street so we don't get caught in bridge traffic," Milo said. "We'll see my contact at the Ministry." As he drove, Milo shared his thinking on other matters. "I am not certain that Tamás Gabor is good for the nation. He comes back to Hungary—big shot, famous, cosmopolitan. His kind of people are bad for us. And where does Gabor's money come from? To whom is this money loyal? And you notice something else? He arrives just when times are bad, when the government will clutch at any straw. When they will *obey*. That is the capitalist way. The Jews' way. I don't trust those people."

2

Chester Holt was waiting for me in the bar of the Hotel Corvinus. I had stopped at my room, changed into dry shoes and a pressed suit, decided there was nothing I could do about the panicked look I saw in the mirror. When I got downstairs, an Old World fellow in a white tie and tails strolled among the tables, violin at his chin, playing soupy versions of *"La Mer"* and Strauss waltzes. Customers who wanted to look Old World partook of strawberries and cream. The place was almost empty. Five years ago, when I had made my previous pass through, the hotel and the city had been thronged with ferret-eyed go-getters—Germans, Swiss, Dutch, Americans—hoping for telecom deals. That tide had gone out. Either the go-getters had lost their money or they had taken it home. Chester Holt was an anomaly, a man who had cash when much of the world was coming up with pocket lint.

Chester was one-half of the couple filling nubby burgundy armchairs. The chairs enclosed an inlaid table that supported a tiny light and a bowl of nuts but no drinks, both of which had gotten chin-high as Mr. and Mrs. Holt listened to the violin: Chester of the three-piece banker's suit, cranberry-hearts bowtie, high-topped black farmer's shoes, two fingers pinching a little glass of palinka. He wore a three-inch crest of white hair and had small features: ears and eyes could have been snatched off an infant, if they did things like that back in Indiana, where he came from. The eyes were set deep and close together, which gave them an appearance of being shrewd.

Then there was the missus: Charity Holt, cushioned in layers of flowered drapery, hair lacquered black, lips painted Chinese red, chin upraised and square. Cascades of skin drooped from the chin, and you could almost see another face in the folds, upside down with hooded eyes. A double rope of pearls hung down her chest. One white hand bore a stone that would have gotten her finger amputated at Milo's szex club.

"Do we have our meeting?" Chester Holt said.

"Not exactly."

They both were in their sixties, joint owners of a tractor engine company back home. They had a manufacturing plant in Guangdong Province, China, and one in Brazil. Both plants also made generators. Chester wanted a bite at the European market, somewhere labor would be cheap. Not bumpkins despite the old boy's shoes. Here in Budapest, the government was coming up short of money. It had postponed its debt and nationalized pensions. The new national financial advisor, Tamás Gabor, was looking for state assets to sell. Chester Holt hoped Gabor would decide to sell cheap and add some tax breaks.

I sat down at the table.

"Do you have my ten thousand?"

"Yes." I pulled out an envelope with the Hotel Corvinus's name in the corner. I handed it to him. "The fellow selling the introduction didn't show. You may want to approach Gabor directly."

"I like to come into a deal with friends already in place," Holt said, then sighed, "when it's possible."

His wife spoke up. "I don't like the way they do business here. When Chester tries to talk money, they change the subject to Franz Liszt, or Edward Teller, or Gabor. It's as if they're too proud to admit they're broke."

Holt stuffed the envelope into a breast pocket. "Where is that man Sipos?"

"He didn't show either," I said.

"Typical." He locked his fingers across his vest.

I sat and pretended I was calm.

I couldn't get away with many lies. When Sipos's body turned up, the police might not look hard for the killer of a small-time go-between, hustler, pimp, nationalist. I didn't know how thorough they would be. If they were the least bit thorough, and learned he had been dealing with a foreigner, an American, they would push a little harder. Which American? And what had he been involved in? Once we got that far, I couldn't pretend I hadn't gone to meet him, because they would find Chester Holt, who knew I had. Then they would learn I had told Chester that Milo hadn't kept the appointment. And by then, the dullest and laziest cop would be getting suspicious.

If they checked me out in New York, they wouldn't believe anything I said after that.

"Would you like a drink, Patrick?" said Mrs. Holt.

"Sure, thanks." I didn't know if I could keep anything down. The adrenaline rush I'd felt cowering in the trees had soured into nausea. I'd caught the taxi a half-mile from the Parliament, and it had dropped me at a hotel several blocks north of the Corvinus. The weather had kept traffic thin, so it wasn't likely that anyone had seen me traveling with Milo. But he could have bragged to someone about his plans.

Holt flicked a hand at a waiter, and I ordered a Dreher lager.

I drank it slowly.

On the other hand, as devious people like to say, the only person who had seen me anywhere near Kossuth Square was the taxi driver. I didn't remember what he or his car looked like. He might remember a man who had said *"Kossuth ter"* with a foreign accent. If the police didn't know about the driver, it was up to me to say where my rendezvous with Milo had occurred.

"There's a time to step up," Chester Holt said. "Time to strike. If I were a young man like you, Patrick, I would make my fortune all over again. Central Europe, Central Asia— opportunities everywhere." He squinted at me, saw a man in his early thirties whose cuffs weren't frayed, who had worked for a good firm on Wall Street before setting out boldly on his own. Solid middle third of the class at NYU, never charged with a crime. The things that counted didn't show on year-old résumés, and he should have known that. We had met less than a week ago, in London, where I had hung out a shingle as an independent investment adviser.

"I'm sure there are opportunities," I said, "but the natives get to the good ones first." I wondered if he would take the hint, save the money he had earned from a lifetime of work. As of this evening, leaving Hungary seemed like a good idea.

"I can out-deal any of these East Bloc sharpies," Chester replied. "Their system lost, remember? I don't care whether they call themselves Socialists now, or nationalists, or the salvation front, at best you get the same kind of technocrats who ran the command economy. It's a mess, anyone can see that."

"If we get rolling here," Holt said, "I may have some other deals for you to look over, Patrick." He'd raised his tiny chin.

"I would be delighted."

He said, "Things may look bad in this part of Europe, but I'm an optimist. I didn't get where I am being a doom and gloomster. That's for losers."

I had got halfway through the beer without throwing up. So for a while I was an optimist too.

Holt and I made plans to get together first thing in the morning, and I took an elevator up to my floor.

In New York, I had believed in optimism until nine months ago when Randy Bremer's nine-billion-dollar hedge fund blew up. Bremer did the only sensible thing and blamed the Wall Street firm that had sold him credit insurance that hadn't covered a collapse of three currencies at once. The Wall Street firm, Magee, Hoffmeier & Temple, had done the sensible thing and blamed a rogue banker on their staff, who had failed to protect the client's interests. Such things were never permitted at Magee, Hoffmeier & Temple.

Nobody said much about the fact I'd had most of my own money in Randy Bremer's fund.

Settling the government's civil complaint took the rest of it, along with a loft in SoHo. It left me with a storage locker full of stuff the government couldn't sell, my passport, and a couple of bank accounts in Paris that I had forgotten to mention. Left unresolved by the feds, who were used to playing the game, was whether a criminal indictment would follow the civil suit.

I still didn't know the answer to that.

Two Lehman bankers I had gone to school with were doing all right on their own in London. If I could pay my own upkeep, I could keep a desk at their office. Sometimes things came in they couldn't bother with.

Chester and Charity Holt came along my third week.

"The guy is a yokel," said Dan Amos, who was flying in and out of the U.K., floating shares of a Romanian-Austrian internet company. "I don't have time to separate him from his money. You may as well do it."

Holt didn't have that much. A few tens of millions to invest. Not enough to get the attention of a serious investment bank. But we met, and he was eager to have someone carry his bags on a short run down to Budapest. It looked good to have an adviser in tow. People took you seriously. "When we're working on a deal, you'll be Mr. Nice and I'll be Mr. Mean," Chester Holt said.

3

Peter Rice was a Central European stringer for a half dozen British newspapers. He smoked cigars and wore a gingery beard that gave him the look of a friendly country parson, quite a large one who needed suspenders to hold up his striped blue trousers. "I've got a trade fair next week in Vilnius," he complained. "I so hate trade fairs. I'm not fond of Vilnius, either."

He lifted a spoon from watery goulash. He alternated mouthfuls of lunch with mouthfuls of smoke, managing a pull at a Czech beer every third or fourth round. I was trying to pump him on Tamás Gabor.

"He thinks he's a philosopher," Rice said. "Made a fortune selling short sterling—you were probably still in your mother's womb then. Press anointed him as a genius for those maneuvers—which really were brilliant, Patrick—and the poor sod read his press clippings, I guess. Set himself up in Switzerland as the man to go to if you wanted to make money in currency trades. Wrote a history of British mercantilism. Pretty good book, all in all."

"But he's not British."

"No, he's Hungarian. His family were secular Jews, made it to London—lucky ones—Hungary didn't deport its Jews till early forty-four. Tamás was ten or so when his parents got out. Some of the grandparents didn't. That's why he set up this Europa Foundation. It peddles liberal democracy as the cure for all ills: just give a Christian or a Muslim a chance to vote and he'll tolerate his Jewish neighbor, that sort of thing."

"What's he doing back home?"

"Spreading wisdom among the unwashed. He tells his countrymen they need a well-balanced economy, not too much capitalism guided by intelligent state direction. To get the debt level down, he has been pushing asset sales. Everybody's trying the same thing, of course, from Greece to Belgium. There are a lot more sellers than buyers."

"China?" I suggested.

"Only until *their* banks implode, which won't be long."

The man sitting next to Peter hadn't said much. He had introduced himself as Andras Kajdi, an editor on a newspaper whose name I couldn't pronounce—it translated as *People's Voice*—and he had written a handful of theatrical plays. He was young and intense and well-dressed. He wasn't eating—another lunch appointment, he said—but had drunk two or three beers with us. "The debt doesn't matter," Andras said. "The only question is how we arrange a limited market economy, how we alleviate human suffering along the way, and how we protect the Hungarian culture."

"You don't 'arrange' a market economy," Peter said. "It arranges itself."

"*Le monde va de lui meme.*" Scornfully.

"Well, you might as well call a spade a spade," Peter said. "I don't pretend I'm for a market economy. I looks at blokes like Patrick here, unprincipled rotters who want to claw their way into the upper classes, which would never have them, and I see that every time me chum Patrick buys a business from the State Property Agency, first thing he does is fire all the workers, them that's given their best years to the company." There was movement under the beard, and I thought he was smiling. "And I ask you, Is that fair?"

Andras had begun nodding, and I understood why Peter kept him around.

"Our problem," Andras said earnestly, "isn't socialism. It's the old fascists. They attracted the worst elements in Hungarian society. There were people in the last government who thought Admiral Horthy was on the right track."

The name was almost familiar to me. "Horthy?"

"Allied the country with the Germans during the Second World War," Peter said. "Ran a little Franco-style dictatorship before that." He shrugged, as if somebody had had to.

Now Andras Kajdi's head was shaking. "Peter doesn't take this seriously. Our nationalism has always had an ugly aspect. 'Hungary for Hungarians,' you know. This is a very Catholic country. There are still a couple of characters in Parliament, way far on the right, who would like to throw out the Gypsies, and the Serbs, and especially the Jews. Is it just coincidence, they ask, that so many Jews had good jobs under the Communists?"

"It was the only game in town," Peter said. "Andras has nightmares about the right wing winning the spring election."

"I'm half Jewish," Andras said.

"Well, for God's sake don't daven at the table," Peter told him, and the younger man looked blank. Peter said, "The main right wing candidate is a brawler, prefers beating people up in the underground to campaigning. I don't really look for his group to go places."

"They're dangerous."

"Where Patrick comes from, they give them radio programs."

"If our fringe were content to talk, I would be less worried," Andras said. He glanced at an expensive wristwatch, apologized and stood up. Wrapped in a dark coat with fur trim, he headed into the cold afternoon. On the sidewalk, he pressed a phone to an ear as he rushed away. He was playing by the town's rules. Act busy. Something might come of it. I debated having another beer. Peter's cigar killed the smell of goulash.

I said, "Where does Andras fit in?"

"He's a social democrat, just like the current crowd in power." Peter chuckled into his glass. "Thinks of himself as a thinker. Rather like Tamás Gabor, now that I mention it." He gave me a sidewise look. "You must know all the Gabor stuff. It's standard fare."

"I thought you might have something new."

"Have your old firm hire me as a consultant and I might find something," Peter offered.

"I don't have any influence at my old firm. Except to get you black-listed."

He wouldn't commiserate with me about that parting. He laid aside the spoon, dunked a thick piece of paprika-laden bread in his bowl. Rust-colored broth trickled into his beard. A paper napkin, lodged over the green knot of his tie, had turned transparent as it became wet. "So what can you offer me in trade? This lunch doesn't cut it, mate. Are your friends in New York in trouble?"

I leaned back. "Trouble?"

"Wall Street's in bad odor. The magic's stopped working."

I nodded, wondered if he actually knew something. Peter had worked in New York until a few years ago. He would still have contacts. Might have heard something. But as far as I knew, I had been the only embarrassment to Magee, Hoffmeier. The firm was conservative by habit. None of the partners got his face on financial TV, and that was the way they liked it.

The problem was, Peter was right. The magic had stopped working. If I let myself, I could see signs of economies around the globe getting worse instead of better. The lines of people without jobs were twice as long in Europe as in the U.S., but the trend was the same: big companies lifting the bridge over the moat, small companies running scared.

"What have you heard, Peter?"

"About your ex-employer, nothing. That's why I asked. In the U.K., there's talk of a capital assessment on large financial companies. You know, take back something from people who've unfairly amassed wealth and spread it around among the deserving poor. I say, 'Right on, comrades!' Time you buggers were made to pay. Don't you agree?"

"I'm paying for lunch," I pointed out.

He dropped his napkin on the table. "It's good seeing you again, despite the lunch."

I walked with him a couple of blocks toward his office.

It was too cold for vendors to have their kiosks open along the Danube, and too gray to appreciate Gellert hegy looming on the river's opposite side. The downriver escarpment supported a monument to Budapest's liberation from fascism, which occurred when the Soviet troops arrived in nineteen forty-five. The liberation from the liberators had taken another forty-five years. I hadn't been to the monument. Milo had said it was a good place to buy drugs. Peter turned south. We couldn't walk directly beside the water because a rail line crowded in there.

"You need a warmer coat," he said. He wore a trench coat, black leather, that fell almost to his ankles. It had shoulder straps, a breast pocket that buttoned, a long belt. Wind was climbing up from the frozen river, but he looked comfortable. He said, "Take a taxi out to Ecseri. You can get a good coat at the flea market for two thousand forint." It was about ten dollars. "They've got thousands of them. The jackets hang in tiers ten feet high."

"Why so many?"

I expected something about the inefficiencies of a command economy.

"The secret police wore them."

"There were a lot of secret police?"

"Still are. But fashions change, and now only the real assholes wear leather."

"I'll watch out for them," I said. "Look—about Gabor."

"What's your interest in Gabor?"

"A client wants to meet him."

"Interested in the foundation?"

"Not in the least."

"Investment business or local stuff?"

"Local, the asset sales."

"I'm glad you've landed on your feet."

"I haven't."

"No?"

"I need this business."

Peter stopped walking, faced me. "You've forgotten the first rule of the financial world. A man fakes it till he makes it. Women, too, but they don't need to be told. Show weakness and your friends avoid you. You're embarrassing and possibly contagious."

"My friends in New York stood by me," I said.

"Did they?"

"Most of them."

"Well, well." He pretended to consider, as a mean grin rose through his beard. He said, "Did any of them line you up with a job?"

I found a bar and dawdled over newspapers. I scoured *People's Freedom* and *People's Voice* for anything that looked like a report of a shooting at the Parliament. The newspapers were both in Magyar, which meant my search was for a photograph of a crime scene or the name SIPOS Milo, which was the local way of putting things. After twenty minutes I gave up. He might still be lying there. Or perhaps the government didn't want to advertise a shooting near Parliament.

Either way, if I had any sense I would cut Chester and his sweetheart adrift, claiming an emergency back in London.

4

Tamás Gabor's offices spread across the second floor of the
Europa Foundation headquarters, room after room, many of
them busy at nine in the evening. The maze was utterly
impenetrable. Charity and I got left at the second or third
perimeter, in straight chairs, along a wall lined with closets.
There was an office on either side of a wide corridor, with glass
partitions through which the nearest clerks could keep an eye on
us. I couldn't tell where the corridor led. Chester had been taken
off through the offices on my right. Charity sat with her hands
on her knees, as if she were about to spring up. She had
congratulated me on my success at the hotel, again in the taxi.
Without looking at me now, she said, "I've got to hand it to you,
young man. . . ."

They were both calling me young man. Peter Rice had come
through that afternoon with a name, which led to another name,
which tied in at the Finance Ministry. "He went to Harvard, just
like you. Happy to phone Gabor," Peter said.

"I didn't go to Harvard," I said.

"I misspoke," Peter said and rang off.

I stretched out my feet, stared at the ceiling. The Europa
Foundation's offices had been modernized only as far up as the
ceiling, which dropped paint flakes.

I heard a door open and two men came through on the
move. Caught up in conversation, they ignored us. One had his
face turned away, all his attention on the pitch he was making to

the man beside him. The talk was in Hungarian, and I couldn't understand a word. The man on the receiving end walked with a patrician air. He was only average height but elegant in a pin-striped suit, his square face framed by steel-gray swept-back hair, a beaky nose supporting rimless glasses, trim blond mustache, unassuming chin. He walked with the ease of a man certain the yapping nuisance beside him would sit on command. They went through double doors at the end of the corridor.

Charity Holt watched them. Her eyes were walnut-sized.

I said, "Does Mr. Holt plan to go home soon?"

"Go home?"

"Indiana."

She gave me a disbelieving stare. "When Mr. Holt and I embark on a project, we see it through."

"I thought the business at home might need attention."

She didn't like it when I was nosy, and she was more likely than Mr. Holt to say so. All I got this time was, "If you have good managers, the business runs well in your absence." Like her husband, she had a weakness for aphorisms. It was supposed to happen to people who spent too much time together, the same kind of talk.

We passed five minutes without more pleasantries. I kept an eye on my watch, wondering when the police would come.

The nicely dressed man with the wire glasses came back and walked straight to us. Thrusting out a hand, he greeted me first. "Patrick McCarry, isn't it? I'm Terrence Innes, Mr. Gabor's executive assistant." His voice was perfect for reading the BBC news. The rimless glasses seemed to disappear on his face. He was ignoring the woman, bad manners even for an Englishman. "Mr. Gabor's absolutely besieged, you know."

"Mrs. Holt's husband is besieging."

"Forgive me, madam. Would you like one of the staff to bring you tea?"

Charity said no, and I said yes because I wanted him to go away.

When Innes had gone into one of the glass offices, Charity said, "Do you think that man is homosexual?"

"I don't know."

A young man brought out a plastic cup of tea. Terrence Innes had gotten busy with a woman pointing at a computer screen. I watched their pantomime until it became boring.

It was ten-thirty when Chester Holt rolled out like a small steam engine, headlight beaming. He swept up his beloved, declared loudly, "I think we're going to do some business," and found a free hand to squeeze my arm. "Mr. Gabor made sure that what we're planning will be good for his country. Jobs and export manufacturing are good for every country! So he turned me over to Mr. Innes, and it looks like there's a site we could use. If it's suitable, and the numbers make sense—that will be your department, Patrick—we can be up and running in three months."

"Congratulations," I said.

"Charity and I will have to inspect the plant. Never buy a pig in a poke, I say." Struggling into an overcoat, he elbowed his wife. "Where do you suppose Baja is?" He pronounced it with a hard "j."

"In the south, dear."

I stopped at the Corvinus's skyway, which straddled Kecskemeti utca, for a brandy. My mood was black. There were plenty of officious people going in and out the front door, and quite a few could be plain clothes policemen. But none of them going in by twos and threes had that hell-bent determined stride of officialdom about to put its foot on someone's neck. The skyway began to fill up with other nightcap drinkers, no more than half of them well-dressed prostitutes.

5

The driver on the trip south belonged to the Europa Foundation and spoke enough English to cry "Don't worry!" every time the back wheels lost traction on a curve. I sat with him in front while the Holts filled the back. The car was a fairly new Mercedes SL, and losing the corners took effort. The driver, whose name was István, was tall and large-boned, with drooping black hair like jagged slats above his eyes. Mustache ends reached an inch below the corners of his mouth, and his chin had both a deep cleft and an array of scars. His "don't worrys" exposed only the lower teeth. His eyes were dark, and it may have been his attention to the icy highway that made them appear homicidal. As he'd climbed into the car after closing the Holts' doors, I'd caught a glimpse of a gun holstered under his left arm. In the two hours and hundred miles since then, I'd thought about the gun once or twice. Hungary wasn't Russia or Bulgaria; going armed on the highways was more luxury than necessity. I wondered if the Holts knew their driver doubled as a bodyguard. Perhaps they had insisted. Chester Holt had started calling the driver "Steve" as we passed Domsod.

The roadside was relentlessly bleak. The wooded areas looked not merely dormant but dead, and scattered conifers were towers of rust. I tried getting a preview of what we would find in Baja, but István couldn't understand my questions and the Holts had a spiral binder open on their shared lap and were inking in amendments to a business plan. I was good enough at

reading upside down to see that the page captions read
MAGYAR TOOL COMPANY.

From a high point in Baja you could see into Serbia, or to the
west into Croatia on the western bank of the Danube. The river
divided here, with the main channel winding south and
marking, more or less, the Croatia-Serbia border, while a branch
that showed up on the maps as Viliki Kana looped into
northwest Serbia. I went down the stairs from the three-story
factory's roof. We were on the southern outskirts of the town
called Baja, and it was gray and shabby and looked as though an
army had moved through, stripping the place before winter set
in, though none had for sixty years.

Our host came right after me, Mihaly Mester, small and
black-haired and saying, "You see? Solid condition throughout."

I didn't bother to ask him what happened when the snow
melted. There were puddles of ice on the floors two levels below.
We got out of the wind, but the interior had been storing cold
since November. The air hadn't brightened Mihaly Mester's
cheeks. They were pale and slack, and his efforts at grinning
intensified the impression he was ill. He was the building's
superintendent, he told me at the gate, and knew Mr. Gabor very
well. I wondered if he lived and slept in the unheated building.

It had plenty of space and was built thick, but I couldn't see
much to recommend the place except, of course, that the border
was just down the road.

"You'll have to bring power in," I told Chester.

"What's that?"

"You couldn't run an air conditioner on the power that's
coming into this building."

"Oh yes." He ambled over to me. I had seen a lot of
lamebrains eager to buy bottomless rowboats—a few had been
clients—and they all wore the same sappy expression
anticipating the pleasures of ownership. Glassy-eyed, see-no-
evil, it's-mine-and-I-love-it. In that mental fog, people bought
waterfront mansions and selected spouses. There was no trace of

JAMES L. ROSS

infatuation in Chester's eye. He knew he was buying a brick pile—buying or going into partnership with, I wasn't sure—and he judged the pile adequate to his purposes. He had already seen the ancient coal-fired furnace on the first level. Asbestos-wrapped tunnels big enough for a man to crawl through connected to two or three ceiling ducts on each level. The furnace didn't work, and the chimney into which it vented had collapsed on the third floor. If we had been in Indianapolis one look would have shown him a black hole in his bank book—tort liabilities, cleanup costs, God knew what—and he wouldn't have been able to get out the door fast enough.

"To make it suitable for manufacturing will cost a fortune," I said.

Mrs. Holt was coming up the stairs almost sideways. Our driver István was nowhere in sight.

"We'll lean hard on that English fellow Innes, and on Gabor. We'll have this dump for a song with an allowance for fix-up. And," Chester smiled, "the government will chip in a bit to train workers."

I inspected the ceiling beams, strolled over to Mihaly Mester. "Show me the furnace again."

He took me downstairs and we clanged open an iron door big enough for a carriage to ride through. I gave it perfunctory attention.

"Work good," Mihaly Mester said, stretching his pallid grin.

I closed the door. The water pipes had been torn out. Work real good. The concrete floor was gritty and oil-stained and showed bolt holes where machinery had once been anchored. The only other evidence of former occupation was a clutter of pipes and trimmed metal against the south wall. I said, "When was the place used?"

He scratched his head. When that didn't help, he waved a hand. "Not long."

"How long?"

He waved at the floor. It was obvious. Yesterday or the day before.

"What did they make here?"

His English wasn't up to that one. He tried giving me the dimensions with his hands. Pretty soon I got tired and went to wait for Mr. and Mrs. Holt. When they came down they wanted to know where István was. I went looking. He was kicking shipping bands along the narrow-gauge rail spur that came into the yard. A couple of saplings growing up between the tracks were an inch across.

"Warm up the car," I said. "The old folks can't stand the cold."

He went to do that, and I intercepted the Holts. "What do you think they used to make here?"

"Mr. Innes tells me it was brooms."

"There's metal scrap on the first floor." I didn't mention the absence of straw or broom poles. I assumed he had noticed.

He made an uninterested noise. The woman shivered. I stood between them and the car. Chester said, "Go ahead, my dear. I'd like to get Patrick's reaction outside Steve's hearing. So, young man? I can tell you're not impressed."

"It's your shop. I don't have to be."

"But I've learned to respect your judgment."

If true, he was on shaky ground. My judgment hadn't warned against meeting Milo in the dark. Not a whimper.

"We can find factory space closer to Budapest," I pointed out. "There would be skilled labor nearby, better infrastructure, rail and highway access—"

"Good points."

He was inviting me to go on. I decided not to bother.

"Here's why I like Baja," Holt said. "We're close to the border. There are good markets for light industrial equipment just south of us, all the way down the Dalmatian coast to Albania. If there's a war, they'll particularly need portable generators. Right now, Serbia buys that kind of equipment from Russia. We'll be able to deliver faster and, with enough handouts from Gabor's ministry, do it cheaper. If there isn't a war, I can undercut prices in most of Central Europe. It all depends on how far the Hungarians are prepared to go to subsidize this project. I'll need your help on that, starting tomorrow." He walked around me, climbed into the Mercedes beside beloved Charity, and István stared out his window daring me to hold them up.

I got in, and he sprayed dust and ice—the yard had no sign of gravel—as the hunched figure of the property's superintendent emerged to shut the gate.

"Patrick's skeptical of the property," Chester told his wife.

She gave me an evil look. "Capital doesn't grow on trees."

Her husband spoke to the back of the driver's head. "Steve, I'm afraid we're not getting much heat back here."

István jiggled the temperature lever. Hot air blew in my face. He tried again, and Chester sighed.

Peter Rice and I had dinner at Gambrinus, where the musicians pretended they didn't know "Lili Marlene" when Peter asked for it. We knocked off three bottles of the local plonk, then two glasses each of Szilva sweet plum brandy, and I let a taxi drop me at the door of the hotel. I was a little tight. Two men had me by the arms before I reached the door.

6

For five hours, they nodded to themselves knowingly each time they told me that a valued Hungarian citizen named Milo Sipos had had a fiancée to whom he had confided his plans. In particular, something about meeting his American friend Patrick McCarry.

"Could you tell me what happened then?" His name was Hruby, the door said *Fohadnagy* Hruby, which was on the order of *Captain,* and he'd gone to a school that taught policemen finesse. He didn't smell of garlic or paprika. He had short brown hair on top and a deep, smile-shaped furrow in his forehead. I guessed his age was in the mid-fifties. He wasn't more than five-ten but wide and thick, and he moved back and forth on the other side of a polished interview table as if conscious of his body's power. Not that long ago Hruby or his predecessor would have done his interviewing at a blood-stained table, if only for symbolism's sake, and its message would have been clear.

Could I tell him what had happened?

"Yes."

His eyes gleamed. "Yes?"

"He didn't show up."

"I suppose you saw no one else?"

"I saw a great many people. It's a busy place. But no Milo."

"The 'busy place'—what are you talking about?"

"A bar at the Forum Hotel. Bierstub Dab, they call it.

Expensive, but Milo wasn't buying." I listened to myself and watched Hruby's face. The message in the shiny eyes was that they could see through liars, who suffered terribly, notwithstanding his country's respect for legal formalities. Listening to myself, I knew my voice was too glib, the answers utterly unconvincing. Hruby couldn't help but see through me.

If I annoyed him, he might decide to hang Sipos's death on me.

He might, but I was going to lie to Hruby with every breath, my face straight and sincere, forcing the dread inside me to stay silent. It was hopeless to tell the truth to the police—maybe not hopeless but not the way to bet. A cop could be as indifferent to the truth as a card dealer or a priest. Hruby might be worse than indifferent, a relic of the old school who had extracted lies by force, insisting on the lie that could become an official truth. He was accustomed to that power, accustomed to sensing fear in the other person. I didn't have to pretend to be afraid. If he got the slightest hint that I had been present when Milo died, my status would change from visiting American national to official suspect, and the interrogation would turn physical and brutal and he would enjoy that so much that the full truth no longer mattered.

I didn't have to pretend to be afraid of him.

He had inspected by passport and my business card. "You work out of London," Hruby said.

"Yes."

"For yourself."

"That's right."

"And you are helping this Mr. Holt on a transaction."

"Yes."

"What sort of help?"

"The financial terms," I said. "Projecting revenues, costs, profits."

"So you are a financial adviser? And that is why you were to meet Mr. Sipos?"

It was past time for an innocent man to suspect something was wrong. I said: "There's a problem with Milo, isn't there?"

"You visited the bar, saw your contact wasn't there, and you left. Is that correct?"

"I waited about an hour and had a couple of drinks. Then I had to meet my client, Mr. Holt. What's happened to Milo?"

There was a pause.

I filled it. "Before this goes any further, I want to call my embassy."

"Of course." He nodded, and a slender man nearby nodded back, but neither of them told me what had happened to Milo, and neither brought me a telephone. Instead, still politely: How long had I known Milo Sipos, how had we met, what was our business relationship, what had I drunk at the Forum, when had I arrived, and so on. I was vague on most of the answers. I had picked up Milo's name from a journalist, a Mr. Rice, who understood he was an intermediary. Who remembers what he drinks?

Hruby got very shrewd and asked if I had spoken with Milo in the last twenty-four hours.

"I've been busy with my clients, Mr. and Mrs. Holt. We drove down to Baja this morning. They want to open a factory." I cleared my throat. "Shall I ask again to call the embassy?"

He bent a heavy wrist, inspected a watch. "No one will be there. It is four in the morning. I must understand your story better. When were you scheduled to meet Sipos?"

"About seven o'clock."

"About, why about?"

"He's never very precise. Nor very reliable."

He formed a trace of a smile. "You are used to dealing with reliable people?"

I didn't answer.

"Why were you meeting him, again please?"

"He was arranging an introduction to Tamás Gabor's people. Mr. Holt was looking for a factory." I'd wondered if the name of Hungary's wealthiest son would impress him. He gave no sign it had.

"But I still don't understand. Why were you meeting Sipos?"

"To find out whether we were wasting my client's time," I said. "Milo promised access. There was going to be a small fee paid to someone—I'm not sure who. When Milo failed to meet me, I assumed the deal was off. I turned the money back to my client."

Hruby was silent for a minute, then said, "Your client must be grateful that you saved him this payment."

"For Mr. Holt it was pocket change."

"And yet your client has met with Mr. Gabor anyway?"

"I found another way in. Old Harvard classmate."

"I'm certain Mr. Holt will confirm everything you've said."

"Of course."

"Yes." He hummed. "I have some very sad news for you concerning Milo Sipos."

The bad news gave him an excuse for going back over the same questions, and an hour later a young woman came in with a message and Hruby left. When he came back, he said I would be able to speak to an embassy officer in person and his assistant took me down to a car.

It was a trick, I thought. They would drive me around the block and bring me back and Hruby would be smiling and ready to demonstrate how he had done things in the old days.

The car was a black Mercedes, and it roared through the night streets in a direction I knew wasn't toward the embassy.

7

Magdalena Glasgow's official status wasn't clear. The first card she gave me described her as a deputy information attaché. Her office was halfway across town from the embassy, up a narrow stairway on Bajza, through a narrow doorway, past a reception desk that nearly filled a tiny foyer. The floors were uncarpeted, the tiles deeply worn. Except for a black-and-white photograph of a since-retired U.S. president, the walls were bare. Square little tape stains and white nail craters marked spots where a previous occupant might have tried to personalize the surroundings. I doubted it had been this woman.

She wore a squiggle-lipped expression that mixed disgust with self-pity. She had a good face for it; was probably wearing a sour pout when she dropped from the womb forty-some joyless winters ago. Her hair was blond tending to gray. Her face was long with grainy pale skin. Only her lips seemed drawn from another face. They were wide and full, and *Elle* could have shot a cover close-up of those lips wearing any shade of red and boosted sales on three continents.

"I didn't know he was in the arms business," I said.

She had been asking me—telling me—about Chester Holt.

"You're just an innocent abroad."

I didn't have an answer to that.

"If you didn't know he sold arms, what did you imagine he did?"

"Engines."

"Engines?"

"For tractors . . . generators."

I sat in the stiff chair in the cold room and wondered how deep in I'd gotten. Magdalena Glasgow didn't make perfect sense. A deputy information officer wouldn't be awake before dawn to take over my care.

I said, "He talks like someone making engines."

"He does make them, in China and Brazil," Glasgow said. "But rocket launchers and machine guns are higher-margin. What has he asked you to do?"

"Help him buy a plant site." She let that sit, so I went on. "The State Property Agency wants to unload assets. Tamás Gabor, the financier, is overseeing the sales." I tried to find something in the office to look at besides the woman's face. The bookshelves lacked books, there were no family photos, no coffee mugs with clever motifs, no tropical plants, no evidence that she had been in residence here more than an hour or would remain more than another hour. The desk was cluttered with paper scraps and faxes, nothing I could read upside down. Behind her, a low cabinet supported a small computer beside a black woven handbag. The window above the cabinet was dark. Hours to go before first light. I said, "If he's in the arms business, why here?"

"I imagine he might think the customers are nearby. Wouldn't you?" She saw that I didn't know and said, "There are two wars about to get going in the region, one just two hundred miles south of where we sit. There is the potential for more, if various ethnic groups reach for their destiny. He could supply Serbia, Macedonia, perhaps Albania, wherever there's a market."

I felt less surprised than I should have.

"The ambassador," she said, "made a phone call two hours ago asking that you be cut loose. He did so after I assured him you work for a reputable firm in New York and couldn't know what Mr. Holt is doing. You see, I did you a favor. If I had told him you were chased out of New York, you would still be in Captain Hruby's custody."

"Why did you do that?"

"Too many details confuse the ambassador. Also, I don't believe you know what Holt is up to. You were sitting in London talking to the pigeons and he came to you."

"You've been watching Holt."

"Of course we watch him." She folded her hands. "The Hungarian government knows nothing about this. As for Mr. Sipos, the police may care—a little—about catching his killer, but I don't. So I wouldn't mind if they charged you with the murder."

"I didn't kill him."

"As I said, I don't care. Captain Hruby probably didn't mention it, but Sipos had ties to a Russian dealer. He set you up. You seem to have Holt's confidence. What do you think he's doing?"

"He's not going to be making weapons parts. Not any time soon."

"How can you be sure?"

"The plant he's going to buy wouldn't support any kind of foundry or stamping mill."

"And if he's bringing in parts from somewhere?"

"He could get an assembly operation going. But not much of one unless he's got a private work force lined up. The population is rural."

"What else have you concluded?"

"Nothing. Suppose you're right about Holt. What does the U.S. care if he churns out machine guns or bazookas? If Budapest doesn't like it, they'll shut him down."

"Perhaps. It might depend where the weapons are going. The government isn't happy about the way some of the neighboring states, such as Romania, treat their ethnic Hungarian minority. This wouldn't be the first government to try to arm an irredentist population next door, stir an uprising that demands intervention. We don't need any more pots boiling in the region." She pushed a business card at me. This was a different one, nothing about assistant attaché, instead the words *Burly Burgers* crowning a plump sandwich and a telephone number across the bottom. "I want you to call this number every six hours and tell whoever answers what the Holts are up to. Who they're meeting. Where they're headed."

"I don't spy on people," I said.

"If Hungary deported you, I'm afraid you would find yourself in New York and possibly under arrest."

"I settled with the government."

"*Please.*" She said it blandly.

"If you're worried about what Chester Holt is up to," I said, "why not have the Hungarians deport him?"

"Mr. Holt is an American citizen, who has certain rights. You don't. I think you want to help me."

A young man that the Ivy League had just scrubbed and tossed into the world opened the door again and this time brought in coffee and sweet rolls. Magdalena Glasgow got down to business. She'd pulled two photographs from under the faxes. "You especially want to watch for this man. His name is James Wilkes. He's the Holts' design engineer." He had a blond crew cut and a snub nose; or the features might have been flattened by the long lens someone had used. He was in sharp focus, and the picture wasn't grainy. I'd had a girlfriend who did photography, and I knew enough to be impressed.

"This person" — pointing to a color glossy — "is Erik with a k Smetana. He's a buyer's agent." He was round-faced and bald, and the picture, which looked like a blown up snapshot, was out of focus.

"A buyer's agent for whom?"

"For anyone. He helped arm the Polish Peasants Party for its coup attempt ten years ago. He's been down in Shqipni for a few months."

"Down where?"

"Albania."

"Is there a peasants party there?"

"No need for one." She stared at the photo as if it held a contradiction. "Smetana's expanded in the last few years. Shipped machine guns into Chechnya. May have gotten a planeload to rebels in Jammu-Kashmir a couple of years ago." She took the photo back. "He arrived in Budapest this morning."

"So if I see either Wilkes or Smetana getting chummy with Holt, I should call you?"

"I may not be at that number. Whoever answers. How far does Holt trust you?"

"Not far, I'd guess."

"That's where you stand with me, too." Her pretty lips curled pleasantly. "Keep in mind, I'm a worse enemy than Holt."

I had breakfast at the hotel's dining room, slept fitfully for an hour, and made it to Ferihegny's old terminal in time for the day's first flight to Paris. It was Air France. I carried one light bag and tried to look like a respectable Frenchman heading home. Grim expression could be from having eaten too much paprika. I bought a bottle of duty free Egri Bikavér and declined the lace squares going for fifty dollars. It was almost time to get on the bus that would travel fifty feet to the boarding ramp when I saw the well-scrubbed boy from Magdalena Glasgow's office. He came flying between the shops in the cramped terminal, blond hair bouncing, necktie trailing. When he saw me, a grin replaced panic. He drew a long envelope from an inside pocket. "Miss Glasgow asked me to give you this."

I didn't take it.

"I'm supposed to help you out."

"Keep tabs, you mean."

"Whatever."

"Get lost."

He tried again with the envelope. It was tan, unmarked. "This may be important."

"Why don't you open it?"

"Wouldn't be proper if it's confidential. I almost forgot. Miss

Glasgow said to tell you there's a problem with your passport in
Paris." His face contorted behind tortoise frames. He wanted to
try a smirk but wasn't supposed to.

"Miss Glasgow's been busy."

"What's that?"

I let it drop. Glanced at a wall clock, wondering if there
would be a passport problem in Amsterdam. KLM had a flight
in twenty minutes. I supposed a problem could be arranged
while I was airborne.

"What's your name?"

"Jeremy Butts, sir. Would you like a ride back to town?"

I cashed in my ticket and tucked my passport inside my
billfold. Jeremy Butts led me out to the parking lot, where he had
a Vectra with an anti-theft bar on its wheel. He revved the
engine. "You didn't check out of your hotel, did you? I'll just
drop you there unless you prefer somewhere else. Mr. Holt was
phoning your suite a while ago."

And how do you know that, I wondered, didn't ask.

Gray apartment blocks and dilapidated cottages from the
Bolshie era flicked past, like dirty ice that wouldn't melt for a
generation. The No. 4 route into Budapest was bleak enough to
make you weep.

8

The envelope that Magdalena's boy had given me was full of downloaded newspaper articles about a financial scandal in New York: old-line Wall Street firm with a rogue banker tied to a hedge fund tied to money-laundering with possible ties to terrorism. No arrests, but the U.S. Attorney was investigating.

Randy Bremer's fund hadn't had ties to money-laundering or terrorism, but an investigation could drag on for as long as Glasgow wanted.

I threw the envelope into a desk drawer.

She had made her point.

Chester Holt tracked me down five minutes later. He had been on my mind. Glasgow didn't want to be seen trampling his rights, but I had no compunctions. If I could get the Holts kicked out of Hungary, Glasgow would have no further use for me. Getting that set in motion might take as little as a word to the police, if Captain Hruby didn't think I was trying to distract him from my own case. If he thought that, he might hang onto both of us.

I had gotten that far when the phone rang and Chester said, "You must be in demand, Patrick! I've been trying to reach you since six a.m."

He wasn't ticked off, but I murmured an apology anyway and said, "Do we meet Innes today?"

"Four this afternoon. I want the upper hand when we talk. The plant isn't worth much, might even have a negative value when you think what it would cost to tear it down. But that's a plus. What are your suggestions?"

I leaned as far back as the wall. He had to be sixty-five, Chester did, and he'd have been squeezing water out of business deals before my mother had ever bedded the better-looking of the McCarry brothers.

"You're going to push for a tax holiday?"

"Of course."

Pup teaching the old bulldog to chew bones.

"Subsidy for rehabbing costs?"

"Splendid! Yes."

"Something for job training."

He had already mentioned that, but responded as if I'd thought it up myself.

I put together a draft of a term sheet and emailed it to Chester. We met in his suite at one p.m., went over the proposal and added a few ornaments. I suggested we ask for a government guarantee against interruptions in the power supply, with penalties if production at the plant got delayed. Chester liked that one.

Terrence Innes fought hard but wanted to be rid of the property. By six that evening, we had about half what we'd asked for, which by my calculation meant that Chester and Charity Holt owned one ramshackle factory free and clear without having put up any money.

"We don't normally let properties go on such relaxed terms," Innes said. "But there isn't much demand for industrial plant that far south." Business done, he played host. "Would anyone like tea?"

"Coffee," said Holt. "I don't normally like to do business with governments, even at one remove."

Charity nodded so vigorously I expected the lacquered black hair to stir. "It invites too many complications," she said.

Terrence Innes forced a smile that showed at least two teeth. "Like it or not, this government remains the prime decision-maker and often the largest customer." As he thought for a moment, the smile disappeared. "If you plan to make generators, you'll find how that works."

I reported in at the number Glasgow had given me, but the voice at the other end, after answering "Burly Burgers," was unimpressed. "This isn't information," he sniffed. "We want you to watch for Wilkes and Smetana."

When Peter Rice showed up at the Corvinus, I was only half-surprised. He phoned my room and I came down to the bar, where he waved a newspaper at me. "What's the name of that chap I steered you to? Sipos, wasn't it?"

"Sounds right." I thought it was safe to show a little interest. "Where did you come up with him?"

Peter was drinking local plonk, Bull's Blood they called it in English, otherwise Egri Bikavér. I had learned a couple of words in Magyar, both of them for booze, and was proud of myself. Peter shook his head. "Andras, perhaps? I can't remember. The town if full of small-time operators. But that's not the point." He lifted a tabloid newspaper. The front page was dense with type. "This rag of Andras's has its share of scoops. They think fascists are hanging like bats from the ceiling. That earns Andras good contacts."

I couldn't read the masthead type or anything else. "What's it called?" I'd forgotten.

"*People's Voice*. Politics like it sounds. The Socialists cornered idealism the year Christ was born, cetera. And it says right here"—he pushed the paper my way—"that a bugger named Milo Sipos turned up riddled with bullets in Kossuth Square. Think he's your bugger?"

"Yes. The police more or less asked if I'd riddled him."

"Regular police?"

"I assume so. The man in charge was Hruby."

He shrugged. "Means nothing. Did they take you in?"

"Yes."

"Where?"

"Not far from the river." I couldn't remember the street. "Gray building like a bank but no columns out front."

"That's the Interior Ministry, *Belugyminiszterium*, on József Attila Street. Green uniforms? That's it. Makes little Andras Kajdi's story more plausible. This piece"—he tapped the headline—"says Milo Sipos was an informant for the secret police."

I picked up the newspaper. Silly, of course. The article could have proclaimed Milo the reincarnation of Buddha for all I could tell.

Peter said, "They couldn't really think you'd shot him or you'd be hanging by your cock in the basement. But they let you go, uhm?"

"I told them I hadn't seen him that evening, and they believed me."

"If he was reporting on you . . . but why you in the first place? What haven't you told Peter?"

"What else does the story say?"

"It's all knowledgeable sources bullshit. The body was found at about, let's see, eight yesterday morning, apparently died with difficulty as a number of holes were in him. State security is heading the investigation. Uhm, that could be the Interior Ministry or the Prime Minister's plain clothes spooks. It will surprise you to learn that Sipos's assignment was the infiltration of the neo-fascist movements. Didn't realize that's where your sympathies lay. We shouldn't be talking."

"It's a bit late. You're already contaminated."

His stare was serious. "You're not political, not at all—are you?"

"Try not."

"It does dilute the fun—choosing sides. You're also in danger of looking like an ass too often. Here's my fellow Socialist brother, Jacob Folkestone, of the League of Journalists back home, accusing Sean O'Beollain of working for the CIA." He skimmed the report, clucking.

"Who's O'Beollain?"

"Minor writer, nobody really, but Jacob's all bothered."

He should meet Magdalena Glasgow, I thought. Said: "That's in the *People's Voice*?"

"The gentlemen, Folkestone and O'Beallain, are both in town, taking opposite sides on press independence."

"Whose side are you on?"

"The common man's. I know he'll take it up the arse, time and again." He looked at his wine, to be looking away from me when he said, "You don't want to mess in local politics."

"I haven't been."

"Don't be sure. It's hard to tell where business starts being political. Pretty early, if not right from the start."

"I'll keep it in mind."

"Good. I've got to take a run up to Belarus tomorrow. Ever been? They're tight with the Russians but miss Stalin. I'd like to find someone to bunk with. Sluch Hotel has two-hundred-year-old rodent shit under the beds."

"I can't help you," I said.

He left me alone, and I forgot about his travel problems. So Milo had died hard, *riddled*. Andras Kajdi's poetic license? It sounded better than saying he'd dropped like a squab on the first shot.

Which I was supposed to have done, dropped on the first shot, after being steered into position by Milo.

I hadn't disputed Glasgow's line about a Russian dealer. But the fact I had been carrying ten thousand dollars might have weighed more heavily in Milo's mind.

I walked around the hotel's public spaces. It was a big spread: ballrooms, shops, business center, gymnasium, art gallery, more shops. A man in a brown suit never got close to me but was seldom out of sight. Hruby's, I supposed.

9

There was a pretty redhead in the bar when I went back. She wore a green scarf and jade earrings and a gray wool dress that looked serious. She was speaking French to a man who could have been ten years younger than she. I recognized the man. Jeremy Butts, he'd called himself. Then I saw past the red wig and recognized the woman's sumptuous lips and the sour look in her eyes and dropped the idea of trying to pick her up.

I sat at the far end of the bar, ordered seltzer and took a matchbook from beside an ashtray. I wrote inside the book: SMET ROOM 522.

I drank my seltzer.

On my way out, I tossed the matchbook in front of Jeremy Butts.

He gave a startled jerk.

I kept walking.

10

Next morning I could spot neither Hruby's man nor any of Glasgow's crew. I was thinking about Peter Rice's travel plans.

He rented space in a stylish, hollowed-out building that had offices stacked around a central atrium, Gothic on the outside, ultramodern in. The skylights were clouded with snow, which made the interior column of artfully shaped air as gray as dusk. I found a porter who accepted fifty dollars to open the door to Peter's office. It was eleven-fifteen. Peter apparently had made his train. I disconnected his telephone from the answering device, noted the number.

I tapped out the number for the Corvinus, asked for the message desk, left six words for Mr. Chester Holt. I dug out Chester's pager number, called it, and entered the number of the hotel desk. It wasn't a perfect test. Chester might not be smart enough to ask for messages. He might get the one I had left and know from the absence of some identifying code that the message was a fake. He might return the call out of curiosity rather than because he recognized the name I had left. The clerk had read the message back to me: SMETANA WISHES TO BE CALLED AT 142-37-17.

I put my feet up and concentrated on nothing.

Ten minutes till Peter's phone rang. I had to make sure. It could have been one of Peter's cronies. I lifted the receiver, said gruffly, through a handkerchief, *"Jo reggelt."*

"Hello?"

"Jo reggelt?"

"Hello?"

"*Jo reggelt?*"

"Oh!" He sounded flustered, but I wasn't certain who it was until he said, "Is there somewhere else I should call you?"

"*Jo reggelt?*"

"*Oh!*" The receiver came down. A wrong number, obviously. He would give the hotel clerk hell, would wonder soon after that if he'd misdialed.

It rang two minutes later. I picked up and muttered, "*Jo reggelt.*"

Chester Holt hung up.

I left Peter's machine disconnected. It was past time to get out of Dodge. I resolved to hit Chester up for my fee but not to hang around if he declined to pay. He would be right to balk: the job was half-done, and my part had consisted of holding his coat. The question was how little I could toss Magdalena Glasgow and still satisfy her. I phoned her at the information office.

"That was not funny last night," she said.

"Quit staking me out. You said Erik Smetana was in town. Where is he staying?"

In silence she went through all the reasons she shouldn't tell me, then got to the reason she should, because knowing would make my job easier. "The Thermal. Has there been contact?"

"An attempt."

I hung up, got a taxi over to Margitsziget, Margaret Island. No tails today, or they were better. It was snowing, and the wind converged from both arms of the river at once. The rose gardens on the island lay barren, and there were only two or three huddled figures in sight on the paths. Walking into the Thermal Hotel, which offered medicinal baths, was a step into everything the twenty-first century could provide to make a high-end hotel feel underpriced. Jeremy Butts was sitting alone on an enclosed terrace sipping something from a steamy glass.

When I sat down, he said with well-bred disapproval, "I'm never in favor of using amateurs."

"You can't recruit the whole Princeton class for this kind of dirty work," I said. It wouldn't improve matters if I pointed out that his tortoiseshell glasses, rep tie and navy blazer marked him unmistakably as an American. I didn't resent his pedigree because his stiffness gave me a clue of the price that came with it. Poor Jeremy might have to measure himself every morning against a father or granddad who had been an unbribeable judge or Wall Street fixture when that counted for something.

"Have you seen Smetana?" I asked.

"No. We've got a floor maid who is supposed to phone me when he leaves his room, or if he gets a visitor. It's a little problematic; she's got other duties. The local talent knows he's in town too."

"Local talent?"

"Secret police. Couple of them are in the restaurant."

"Do they know you?"

"They may know I'm with the embassy." He sipped whatever he was sipping. It smelled like Chinese bath water. "By the way, Miss Glasgow says you're supposed to provide information to us, not the other way around."

"What do you want to know?"

That flustered him. "What have you come up with?"

"Nothing."

He went back to his drink. "You messed up back in the States, according to Miss Glasgow. I hope you don't mess up this operation."

A portly man in a blue hotel robe wandered near the table, looking for the baths. A woman as old as the riverbed crept along on two canes.

"I was thinking of visiting Smetana," I said. Stirred in my chair.

"You're not cleared to do that," Jeremy said. "Let me tell you two things. *Primo*, you don't want to annoy Miss Glasgow. *Secundo*, you don't want to *piss off* Miss Glasgow." He gave me a look, decided it was worth a try, and said, "And for purposes of this surveillance, pissing me off is equivalent to pissing off Miss Glasgow."

I like people who say things like *primo* and *secundo*. I said, "I think I'll go see him anyway."

He struggled not to spring out of his chair. "Don't do that!"

I stayed seated. We both did.

"You need to develop a poker face," I said.

"I know."

"I don't know what the big deal is."

"You don't have to know. All you have to do is not screw it up."

"Difficult, you know, when one lacks the larger picture. Do you know why Smetana is in town?"

"I can't discuss this."

He didn't know. She'd sent him out to baby sit, to collect contacts, but hadn't given him Erik Smetana's full c.v. I said, "He supplies arms to anyone with a few aid dollars left over."

He was being fairly attentive to people passing through the lobby. He said, "So do a dozen people we don't care about. If I were cynical, I might think he's a competitor of someone we like better. But I would never say that."

Most of his attention was on the lobby. The elevators were on the other side, but logically anyone heading in or out should pass within Jeremy's range—unless the person didn't want to be seen. Then there would be a service elevator.

Smetana could be in his room, hosting the local gun show for buyers from Macedonia to Albania. I started to say so, but Charity Holt stalked in from outdoors, shedding snow. She headed through the lobby, where I lost track of her.

I got up. "I'm going to hit the head. You can come along. But it would look suspicious."

The house phones were on sandalwood pedestals. I asked for the front desk, told the woman who answered, "This is Mr. Holt. Would you inform Mr. Smetana that I'm *still* waiting in the lobby."

Smetana and Mrs. Holt wouldn't be clumsy enough to come down themselves for a look. I went back to Jeremy at his table. "Let's order dessert, it'll look better."

That worried him—*What* would look better?—but the waiter came back almost immediately with two pots of fragrant bath water and a *pgacsa* pastry assortment. It was less than another minute before two men in good western suits appeared with topcoats and suitcases and the weary routine of businessmen on their last legs and began giving the lobby a close going-over. If they'd come from outside it would have been more plausible, but there hadn't been time and there was no snow on their hair or shoes. With my back to the show, I let Jeremy describe it. We were having a lively conversation, like old buddies from the diplomatic circuit catching up on the good postings. The two businessmen came through from the lobby, set up at a table fifty feet from us, and looked at everyone. I'd expected them to go once around, then head upstairs to report that nobody was in sight pretending to be Chester Holt. Someone had figured out that the only reason for the call was to smoke out the other players, and they were wondering who would do that.

Leaning into it, Jeremy said, "What the hell are you trying to accomplish?" He said it with a smile. Two chums from Woodie Woo. Say, did I remember what's-her-name who slept with *everybody*?

It was something you couldn't avoid when you were hustling a deal, or buying a currency, you wanted to know who else was in the game, were the big names on your side or the other side? So you made a little noise, made a couple of feints, and pretty soon if you were buying something somebody else was trying to buy, the other player showed himself.

"Do you recognize them?" I said.

Jenny Weinglass. Cooked like an angel, fucked like the devil. Great girl.

"No."

"Where would you guess they're from?" I said.

The whole rowing team?

Yeah, that Jenny.

They were in the wrong place for Jeremy to have another look without being stupid about it. He settled for impressing me with how much he had noticed the first time. "Suits look American. The shoes are Allen-Edmonds, I'll bet, though they could've been Church's."

Jacob Weinglass's little girl?

Both men had hair combed straight back like wet tar. That ruined the effect of the suits and the shoes. They didn't seem to be watching anybody at the moment.

"Here's the problem," I told Jeremy. "There's somebody upstairs visiting Smetana who can recognize me. In a few minutes, she's going to make an appearance because she's going to want to know what's going on."

"Who is it?"

"A dancer from Dolce Vita. I saw her come in fifteen minutes ago."

"What's she got to do with Smetana? What's her name?"

"How would I know? You're the professional. She called herself Katona."

"What's she look like?"

"Blond, blue-eyed, thighs a little thin. I called Smetana's room and asked for her."

"Oh, brother." He glanced at the doorway, couldn't help himself.

"How's your Hungarian?" I asked.

"Passable."

"For New York or Margaret Island?" It wouldn't be good enough if they were fluent. "Any other languages?"

"My French is quite acceptable in Paris."

Nobody's French was acceptable in Paris. But his would have to do. "When I get up and leave," I said, "you're going to babble at me about poor dear François, whose paintings are too far ahead of their time, and then you're going to sit here and speak nothing but French to the waiters and hope our friends buy it." Before he could object, I added, "The alternative is, I'm going to be made by the tart from Dolce Vita, who knows I'm American, and if I'm American you're probably one too and they're going to be halfway to blowing you and Miss Glasgow."

"They wouldn't be if you—"

"Shh. Think of Jenny Weinglass."

"Who the hell is that?"

Unless they were absolute idiots, they wouldn't buy Jeremy in his Brooks Brothers blazer as a Frenchman, but disbelief might take long enough to get me off the island in the clear.

If I got out the door before Charity Holt came down.

He gave me a look that said these matters would be brought to the attention of Miss Glasgow, or the dean's office. I got up.

"You're on, Maurice."

11

"They gave your office to a former nun," Timothy Upham said.

We hadn't talked in four months, hadn't seen each other in almost a year. He had been wary until it was clear the McCarry taint wouldn't spread to the rest of the building at Magee, Hoffmeier & Temple. Now he sounded busy.

"A nun," I said. I hadn't expected management to leave the desk empty as a warning to recruits of how a career could die. I wasn't sure what I had imagined. I kept backing away from the knowledge that my former life was over, with finality, really and truly *gone*. People abandon New York all the time, and from a waterfront table in the south of France, where I had spent part of one summer, exile might have had its attractions, the next chapter begins and so forth. From a shared space in London, or an iced-in stone building in Budapest, it was akin to leaving the sleek and clever girl for the dull one with hair on her ears.

"A nun?"

"Former nun. Calls herself Rusty. None of us has learned what her name was when she was married to Jesus. Tough gal, not bad looking, already arranged the sale of a genealogical tech company to Google." He whispered, "You think she's tied in with the Vatican?"

"Or the Mormons," I suggested.

"I can't help wondering what she would be like on a date." He had a wife and, last I'd heard, a sometime thing with a broker trainee.

I cut him off. "Do you think you could pull a full Bloomberg profile on someone for me?"

"Who do you want?"

"Tamás Gabor."

"Ho, big time."

"Also—" I gave him the names Holt Industries and Chester Holt.

"No problem. Tell me what you're doing these days. You've still got friends who wonder."

Staring at the icy air outside the bar where I'd settled in, I gave him the broad outline and he wished me luck and promised to email whatever he could within an hour.

The Holts weren't the king and queen of Saturday night specials in Indianapolis, I saw reading their D&B that Timothy Upham sent. Their company made small engines, mostly used in portable generators, some in lightweight tractors, the sort you would mow a lawn with. That replaced my image of a behemoth dragging a plow across Middle Western barley fields, or whatever got grown in the Middle West.

Two other small subsidiaries ground castings and repaired diesel engines. But Magdalena Glasgow hadn't kidded me, not completely. There *was* a gun business. Five years ago, Holt Industries had bought the assets and name of a bankrupt Belgian manufacturer of military rifles and machine guns. The subsidiary's name meant nothing to me, TACEM. According to D&B, the unit was still believed to be operating at a loss on declining sales to NATO armies.

TACEM could use new customers.

The Bloomberg's articles made Tamás Gabor the toast of London and Paris, which I already knew: investor, philanthropist, firm friend of peace and democracy. His fourteen-billion-dollar Euro Partners Fund had returned forty-two percent to its investors last year, even as its master devoted himself to his homeland's problems. It took an unusual man to make four billion or so working part time. I was admiring and curious. A photograph made Gabor look like a coal miner with the mange, big and swarthy, a button-popping chest, whispy hair and a walrus mustache, fists on his hips, boots planted atop a mine tailings pile. From the picture you couldn't tell for sure whether he was six-four or five-five. But he looked big. Big man, big money, big confidence. None of the reporters who had written the tributes had gotten to interview the man.

If Gabor *lost* forty-two percent of his investors' money, the fawning journalists would turn around and gang-bang him till he couldn't walk.

A London paper put in dates and details. Tamás Gabor had left Hungary in nineteen fifty-seven, the year after an anti-Communist uprising was crushed. He had made a small pile as a stock broker while winning honors in economics and philosophy at the Sorbonne. I got tired of reading by the time Tamás was twenty-eight and was worth more than five million. The writer's point was that you only needed to liberate human talent from oppression to see it blossom. Peter Rice would have bowed to the sweet sentiment and observed that oppression *was* a human talent.

Something bothered me about what I'd read. Peter—or was it Andras Kajdi?—had left me thinking that the Gabor family had fled Hungary during World War II, before the Germans took over. This article said he'd gotten out more than a decade later. That would have put him in his early twenties.

I ate dinner alone at the hotel. I didn't know where the Holts had gotten to and hoped they wouldn't hurry back from wherever it was. I'd barely tasted the wild boar soup when a wheelchair rolled into the dining room. The man in the chair, blond and crew cut, had a blunt nose, just as in the photograph Glasgow had shown me, but he looked older. Glasgow hadn't mentioned that the weapons business's design engineer worked from a wheelchair. The man a step behind the chair was Erik Smetana. They got a table, ordered and talked with the stiff backs of business acquaintances rather than friends. The Holts didn't join them.

12

He showed me a card that said *Burly Burgers*, vice president named Sampson, an empty young face to match, and wasn't I in the investment business, friend of so-and-so in London, and why didn't we have a drink in the bar 'cause he was new to Budapest and maybe I could give him some pointers.

I moved away from the Corvinus's message desk. There was a folded red sheet of paper in the slot bearing my room number that I pretended not to have seen. I told Glasgow's new man, "It's pretty late. Why don't you call me tomorrow."

He put a hand on my upper arm. "Now."

I didn't move.

"We need to talk," he said.

"You need," I said, "to take your hand away."

His eyebrows went up. The Burly Burgers card was supposed to give him nudging rights worldwide, like an American Express card. He said, "Do you know who I am?"

I took his wrist, pulled it gently sideways till it left my sleeve, and let go. There was no resistance in his arm because he wasn't looking for a public brawl.

"I'm not here this time of night," he said, "for the fun of it."

"Tell Maggie I'm off the payroll."

His pale face showed shock as the name "Maggie" registered. None of her boys would ever call her Maggie. He focused on my left lapel and whispered, "You haven't been doing yourself any good. And I don't know who put a bug up your ass, but *we do need to talk.*"

His sense of urgency was contagious, but I told myself to ignore it. What was urgent to Maggie and the sculling team wasn't urgent to me. The players—Smetana, the wheelchair jockey Wilkes—were showing up too fast, and I didn't know how many others Glasgow hadn't mentioned, any or all of them apt to consider me in the way. If I couldn't fly to New York or Paris, the Eastern Station in Budapest had trains to the Czech Republic. I wouldn't be any closer to home, but I would be out of the action. Even if Chester hadn't paid me. . . .

"We may be too late," Sampson murmured.

Through the wide front doors, I saw a car that had pulled under the portico was disgorging men in uniform. There were three of them, each tall and mustached. The uniforms were different from the security force's, blue instead of green. They came through the doors double-time, and I felt Sampson putting distance between us. They glanced every which way and headed straight to the registration desk. They got what they wanted and passed us on the way to the elevators. Either they hadn't had my description or they were looking for somebody else.

Sampson sidled over to the desk, acting chatty, and then decided it was safe to come back. "They're cracking down on prostitutes," he said.

"You'd better get out of town," I told him.

"You're still in trouble. Smetana is nervous about you."

"How do you know?" Then I laughed at myself. By the time Jeremy Butts had recruited the maid, someone else would have bugged Smetana's room, telephone and toothbrush. I said, "So what if he's nervous?"

"Having you killed could calm him down."

I couldn't think of an answer.

"And quit trying to screw up our operation," he said. "This is serious. You don't have the full picture."

Neither did he, I was ready to bet. I waited till he was out the door and into the office Vectra before going to the desk and collecting my message.

The police hadn't reappeared when the young woman with the audio equipment flew out of the bar and said it was her message I was holding, and if we were going to do it we'd better *do* it, didn't I think? She was bright-eyed at eleven-fifteen in the evening, when most decent people were nodding over peach brandy. She kept glancing at the sound meter of her tape recorder. "The people I talked to said you're one of the top free lance deal makers in Budapest," she said by way of buttering me up. She had short brown hair with a few strands of blond or gray; the Corvinus had turned down the lights in the Liszt Bar to give the remaining prostitutes better working conditions, so it was hard to tell hair colors or much else. Most of the tiny windowside tables were occupied. All I could see apart from reflections were walls of snow that enclosed the sidewalks.

"You know NPR?" she said.

"Is it a stock?"

"It's a radio network."

"Oh."

"In Washington." She sounded like she'd just flown in, businesslike, in a hurry.

"I see."

"And I'm Deborah Wolfe, a correspondent. We're doing a series on how Eastern Europe is coping with the world financial crisis."

"Who told you I would know anything?"

"Mr. Innes at the Europa Foundation." She was young enough that anyone in his forties would be mister. "He said your reputation spoke for itself."

I wondered if Innes had done enough checking on New York to be droll. "How nice."

The absurdity wasn't lost on me. The ink was still wet on my letterheads back in London, but here I was an out-of-towner and automatically had credibility. I knew stock brokers who exploited the phenomenon ruthlessly. An investor in Pittsburgh getting a cold call from the local branch of Merrill Lynch might not care. But tell him the broker was calling from Boston or New York and he would feel special. He wouldn't know that Pittsburgh was the New York broker's "model city," defined as a zip code with dollars that need to be scooped out, and that every dentist, chiropractor and plastic surgeon in town was getting the same call.

We got drinks and I wondered if the name McCarry would eventually click with her. If it did, her story could be *Guess what's become of last year's scoundrel?* She lifted her glass and asked how big a deal I was working on.

"Not big," I said, and pointed to the recorder. "I'd rather be off the record."

She switched off. "It's amazing how often I've heard that today." She tilted her drink, just as a couple of girls at other tables did. It was a space filler while the customer thought about the elysian pleasures that could be had for twenty dollars. Deborah Wolfe said, "I really was hoping to interview Mr. Gabor."

"No luck?"

"Too many assistants in the way. You'd think if anyone had a handle on business over here, he would. But there wasn't time today or tomorrow, then he goes back to London."

"Did you try Morgan Stanley?"

"And got the party line. Hungary is going to recover, foreign investment will come back. No debt default. No bank failures. No regression to the bad old days."

"You don't believe it?"

She frowned. "I'm not sure I believe *anywhere* is going to recover. I have trouble trying to explain this on the air. But suppose you had inherited a bank that your great-great-grandfathers built. It was stuffed with centuries of profits. But now, the money has all been spent. You've blown the whole bankroll."

"You think that's Hungary's situation?"

"I think it's the world's situation, in varying degrees. I don't see how countries that have spent so much and borrowed so much will recover."

"Build another bankroll?"

"That takes time. Generations. People in democracies want to be happy and prosperous *today*. Well, people everywhere want that, but *we* can demand it, and politicians have to deliver. It's like a basic right. If we don't get what we want, we start to doubt the system and look for alternatives. Take to the streets. Europe is used to doing that. Hitler was *elected*. Did you know that?"

"I may have heard it. You think things are going to get that bad?"

"I don't know. I don't think anyone does. That was something I wanted to ask Mr. Gabor."

"Wouldn't he tell you he's here to straighten things out?"

"Probably. I would tell him I've seen the numbers on the economy. GDP is down fifteen percent in the last four years. Unemployment's *way* up, likely to stay that way because who wants to hire some doof who's worked for a state enterprise all his life? I talked to the economics minister yesterday. He said the transition has been painful but things are looking up. You know what I think?"

"No."

"I don't think they really *made* the transition."

I didn't say anything.

"Look. If you spend fifty years cutting off people's legs and then tell them to get up and run, they're not going set any course records, are they? And that's what you've got to do today, be better and faster than everyone else."

I looked out the street. The shops were closed, lights off, but I knew they were there, mostly mom-and-pop stores, small restaurants, and near the hotels lace and crafts shops. A few blocks away there was a commercial district, everything from crystal to designer suits. The people running those businesses, and starting new ones, hadn't had their legs cut off. I said, "I don't think it's that bad. Have you taken a walk down Vaci utca?"

"This morning. Bought a scarf in the Labirintus. So what? It's all retail. That's the last thing to go." She smiled sideways. "Women are buying scarves in New York."

Sitting near her was like sitting near a window that was letting in a draft.

"So what's *your* project?" Wolfe asked.

"Rehabbing an old factory."

She looked as if she couldn't believe I was *that* small time.

"You're not very helpful," Wolfe said. She polished off her drink, packed her equipment, and surveyed the long, narrow room. "Maybe I should interview a working girl."

I walked her down to the front door. She got into a taxi, and it pulled away, and across the street the lights of a parked BMW came on and it struggled away from the curb into the snowy ruts and the hotel lights bathed the face of the driver, the firm-mouthed, dedicated profile of Jeremy Butts.

I went up to my room. It was impossible to tell, truly impossible, because if they were clods they were nevertheless professionals and I wouldn't know where to look. I lifted the telephone receiver, punched two digits for the message desk, and listened to the background noise that sounded like an open drain. I didn't know what a wiretap sounded like. All the phones I had used in Europe sounded like drains.

If Glasgow's boys were keeping watch on me, it was fair to assume they had also put some electronics to work. Which explained how Jeremy had gotten after me at the airport.

A mature, businesslike voice piped up in my head. Every bond or stock trader has one; every banker who can read a ledger. It's the voice that says this isn't going your way and you'd better cut the losses. That was what mine was saying.

So why wasn't I packing?

I called the front desk, left a message for the Holts that I would be occupied the next day, might have to return to London on short notice.

Somewhere that evening, Magdalena Glasgow picked up the same message.

I came out of the bathroom bright and early, rubbing my head with a towel. The policeman at the door wore a green uniform and wanted my passport. "Until our investigation into the matter of Milo Sipos has been completed," he said. "Your embassy has been informed."

He couldn't kid me. Maggie had yanked my chain.

I gave him the passport without a word. He was broad-shouldered, formal, impervious to scorn. He said, "Captain Hruby hopes you will enjoy Budapest."

I closed the door and phoned the official number Glasgow had given me. The man who answered could have been Butts or Sampson or another recruit. He took a message and she called back in five minutes. Denied having anything to do with the police visit.

"They must have a stronger suspicion you were involved," she said. "If they charge you, we can't do much. String pulling has its limits. And you haven't been helpful."

"Your string pulling is first rate. Mine feel tighter this morning."

"If we can give Hruby something more interesting," she said, sounding pleased, "he might be grateful."

A tug and the right arm rises. A twitch and the left foot stomps. A tug and a twitch, and the fool dances to your tune.

I thanked her for the pointer, but irony was as wasted today as scorn. When they have you dancing, they don't care how pissy you get.

I took my time getting dressed, had breakfast with a roomful of KLM employees on the mezzanine, and got halfway across the lobby before noticing I had picked up a shadow. From three steps behind me, Sampson came up and said, "You look like a man with an improved attitude. There's a car waiting."

He told me the big news in France was a bank that had lost a few billion Euros trading Italian debt. We agreed it sounded familiar. He had seen a small item in the *IHT* about a worse scandal in Hungary.

"What's that?" I said.

"Rumors of iron oxide contaminating the paprika. They blamed a British food company's agents."

Thinking of the goulash I'd eaten, I said, "How would anyone notice?"

"People get testy about their national treasures, and paprika's one of them."

So were Egri Bikavér, Tamás Gabor, Gabor's brilliance, and broken down factories where they once made brooms, bent metal or roosted pigeons. So were embroidered dresses and tablecloths—God forbid Charity Holt should ever appear in one, or either—national treasures all. And Catholicism, and the uncontaminated Magyar countenance.

13

The blood froze as fast as it flowed.

It was my blood, so I paid attention. Five minutes had passed, and nothing was dripping. The fingertips of my right hand had large carmine pebbles hanging from the ends. The fingers were uniformly red below the middle knuckle. The little finger was lower than the others and had a bright red stalactite hanging from it, translucent in the sunlight.

I rested my head against the door frame. The air had numbed my face. Now the cold was keeping me from fainting.

The car was tremendously bright inside. The windshield was gone except for small crusty wedges. The first shot had taken it out. The near side window was scattered in ten thousand pebbles across my lap and the floor. That had been the second shot.

Sampson appeared at the driver's window. His previously dull face wore streaks of pink and red near the hairline.

"I'm leaving," he said.

It may have been a head wound. He wasn't thinking clearly.

I said, "I know who did it." Not really, but I didn't want to be left alone. Of less interest to me, if he set off I didn't think he would get far. "The car that passed us fifteen minutes ago, the Suzuki, he was hurrying to get ahead and set up." I moved my right arm. It felt stiff and bruised around the shoulder. There was no feeling at all below the elbow. "There must be a side road near here. Do you see a hill?"

The highway had been clear in both directions when the windshield exploded. A rifleman standing along the roadside would have been visible for miles. The shots had to have come from cover, probably from elevation. I didn't know about shooting at cars, but I knew about snowballing them from a height.

There were long-skirted pine trees and brush between us and the road. Not enough trees for my money, but Sampson was standing up as if none of that mattered. Head wound. The hill had to be on the west side of the highway, because it was the passenger's window that had blown on the second shot. But where was the road the Suzuki had taken to reach the shooter's perch? A lot depended on that. I thought five or six minutes were gone, but I didn't know if I had been unconscious. It might be more than five or six. Sampson had driven us among the trees, well away from the highway, by luck or instinct. But that wasn't going to help us for long.

He was supposed to be a pro. Was supposed to be thinking. But in his short career playing spook, he might never have been shot at. As a clay pigeon I had him beat hands down.

"*Did you see a side road?*" I demanded.

"What are you talking about?"

"A turnoff before the shots. Did you see one?" The shooter would be in the Suzuki now, heading down that road, and I didn't know how long we had.

"I haven't been paying attention to side roads," Sampson said.

Okay, if we didn't know where the road was, or the hill, there was no way to estimate how far the Suzuki needed to come or how long it would take.

I spoke patiently. "He was up on a hill, had to be or he'd have followed up by now. Is our car visible from the highway? He knows what he's looking for."

His eyes focused. It was sinking in.

"I don't suppose," I said, "you've got a gun."

He hadn't, of course. He said, "I plan to flag a car on the road."

"Swell. Go ahead. But first—see if you can open this door." It was clear of the tree bottoms and heavier brush, but the handle was below my dead arm.

He stumbled through the snow, looked with pale understanding at my sleeve. Most of the damage I could avoid seeing. The cuff was decorated in colored jewels. The upper sleeve had to be torn, better not to look at that. When the door was open, I brought my feet into the snow and heaved off the seat. Sampson put out a restraining hand as a gesture. He looked ready to step aside if I fell.

"Rub snow on my face," I said.

He did and it helped.

"Did a bullet hit you?" he said.

"Yes."

"You'd better sit down."

"He's going to be here." He or they. If it was they, we didn't stand a chance.

He considered. "We should find cover."

I started down the slope away from the car. The area just ahead looked marshy: tall dead grass sticking out of flat snow that probably covered ice. Sampson came after me, then glanced back. "We're leaving prints."

The problem was, we weren't leaving them fast enough. The snow was calf deep.

Several cars had passed on the road.

How long?

The marshy area was a big low bowl, with sparse trees and bushes on the eastern rim. I tramped across a hundred yards, heading for the trees, not looking back. With the noise I made breathing and stomping, I couldn't hear the road.

The day was just dazzlingly bright. The temperature couldn't be more than ten Fahrenheit, and a little breeze skittered ice crystals across the surface of the snow and made the air colder.

Another fifty yards and I was at a scrim of brush.

He should have arrived.

One of the cars that had passed might have been the Suzuki. He should have spotted the bruised Vectra on the first pass. He would have a close idea of where we had left the road. But if he was in a hurry, wasn't too professional—what did I know about the assassin profession, my only previous experience was with a rodent-faced robber? But he might have overrun the spot and, say a mile down the highway, admitted he had to turn back. So he would be getting back now, seeing the wreck through the trees.

I stopped for breath, and Sampson stopped five steps behind me. Neither of us was wearing boots. He had wanted to scope out the neighborhood around Holt's factory, strictly a driving tour unless nobody was home and he could get past the gate. His pea coat had been too heavy in the car. My topcoat was too light out here. I should have followed Peter's advice, gone shopping. . . . My mind was drifting. The cold was spreading from my arm across my back. It wasn't going to take long.

I realized I had screwed up since leaving the car. We could have gone fifty feet through the roadside trees and circled back to cross the highway, lying low beneath the road's west shoulder. If the shooter followed our trail, we would have had a chance at his Suzuki.

We had gone too far this way, were committed. He was back there now, had to be.

Sampson crouched and looked back at the furrow we had cut. "Would you follow a trail that clear?" he said.

I didn't know.

"I don't think I would," he said, as if he'd had years of man-hunting. Varsity stalking against the Crimson. We scrambled up a gentle slope to the edge of the trees and he said, "Better get your head down. You're not fit to do more walking, that's for sure."

I sank to my knees, then got up and scrambled another ten feet away from the brush line. The ground was a bit higher. The road had dipped where we went off, and we had come up the side of the bowl. I scooped a depression beside the naked-looking skin of a birch and sank into it. Sampson scooted fifty feet to the right. I knew his thinking. He was closer to the highway, and if our friend crossed the bottom in a straight line, Sampson might have a chance to angle away through the light cover.

I tried to hear anything from the road. It was impossible to tell if anyone was stopping. A truck coming from the north provided a flicker of white through the trees. Once it was past, its engine noise dopplered down into the low registers.

If the shooter had come back, he wasn't far behind us, set up against a tree, waiting for movement.

The ground was sapping my body heat. It was a matter of minutes before my shivering became the uncontrolled rattling of hypothermia.

I saw a brilliant flash—sunlight off a scope lens—an instant before he stepped into sight. My subconscious had expected someone who looked like a hunter, in a cap with earflaps and a blaze orange vest over a plaid coat, very specific, leather gloves, green-walled gum boots, rifle at present-arms. After all, he was a hunter.

The long topcoat made him less plausible. The coat hung open over a business suit, red necktie and sparkling white shirt, no sign of boots as he lifted his feet, the gun carried one-handed behind the trigger guard, pointing straight up like a staff.

My impression, when the Suzuki passed, was of one head. But I hadn't been trying to see, and the glimpse had lasted no more than a second after which the sunlight was on the windshield and the vehicle ahead was a silhouette. But I'd thought one person.

Even if I was right about that, there could have been a second car.

As he struggled down into the bowl, I waited and nobody joined him. He was having as hard a time, holding his rifle aloft, as I'd had with a dead arm. It tended to unbalance you, stepping forward and down into snow that gave way to different depths, with only one movable arm. When he was looking at his feet, I risked lifting my head an inch and looked toward Sampson. All that was visible was a blot of navy coat.

The gunman was at the bottom of the bowl now. He was close enough that I could recognize him. I had thought so as soon as he came between the trees, the bright glasses and the mustache and the air of tidiness getting disheveled. I lay there, brain almost as numb as my flesh.

I put my face down on the packed snow, realized I couldn't feel the cold. When I lifted my head, Terrence Innes hadn't made much progress. He had the rifle pointed dead ahead and a hand cupped above his glasses, trying to block out the glare. The effort was useless. He was getting as much light reflected from the snow as direct from the sky. His lenses weren't tinted. The snow field would make him feel exposed, blind to whatever lay in the shadows outside the bowl. He wouldn't know that neither of us was armed. For a minute I let a hope grow that he would lose his nerve. It depended on whether he was an office boy or experienced at this sort of thing. Which way it depended I couldn't decide. An office boy might plunge ahead when an experienced stalker turned back. Or his stalking experience might consist of hunting rabbits and doves, he could be that kind of Englishman on weekends, and one always slogged ahead, didn't one.

He slogged ahead. The track we had left led directly to me, give or take ten feet, close enough that even snow-blinded he would be able to identify a shivering back. I had been too dull-witted to understand why Sampson had moved away. Or perhaps too tired to ask myself, and too tired to follow suit if I got an answer. Being fifty feet away wouldn't make much difference, once Innes got up here with his rifle. I would be first. Sampson would try playing hide and seek through the brush until the rifle brought him down.

Innes was halfway up the slope when Sampson moved. He rose to a crouch that left him all but invisible from Innes's level and pounded in the direction of the highway. Innes ran up the slope. There wasn't any real shade under the bare trees, nothing to confuse the eye, and he had a clear shot and was competent with the rifle. He got off a single round, and Sampson fell and then Innes's feet went out from under him. He landed on his elbows, and the gun discharged again. He was looking straight at me then, about six feet away, squinting over rimless glasses that had come off one ear and hung over the tip of his nose. I scrambled forward with one good hand through last year's berry vines, heaved myself onto the rifle as Innes slid away down the glazed slope. His fingers left the rifle stock. He flailed once, then gave up that idea and dove a hand inside his topcoat and brought out a pistol. I flattened myself and wiggled backwards, dragging the rifle, until I was behind the tree. It was impossible to hear anything that might be going on over my breathing. I clamped my mouth shut. There was a loud pounding pulse but no crunch of anyone coming up a brittle slope.

I tried to make sense of the rifle. There was no bolt to work, no pump, only a flat button to the left that might have been a safety, and a trigger, and a short black clip that probably didn't hold many rounds. I sat beside the tree, held the rifle against the trunk, and sighted through the scope at an out-of-focus bramble ten feet away. I squeezed the trigger, and the stock kicked my shoulder and my ears went a little deaf. Where the slug went I had no idea. I was aiming low. The shot served its main purpose by keeping Terrence Innes's head down.

When I could hear again, he was breathing and moving around. I watched the rim of the depression. He might be confident enough of his marksmanship to think he could pop up where I wasn't looking and pick me off. He might be right. The scope wasn't sighted for ten feet, and even if I'd had a clue how to adjust it I couldn't have stood the distraction. It worried me that he didn't bother talking. Nothing to say, if there had to be only one outcome. But he didn't bother kidding me along, didn't play psychological games, didn't invite me over to his side, whatever it was. He was satisfied having me know he was going for the kill.

The rifle was too heavy to hold aloft with one hand. But I couldn't lie flat and aim at a particular point along the edge because when he came up elsewhere, especially if it was to my right, I wouldn't be able to shift in time. I compromised by standing the gun on its butt with a forward tilt. When it was time to let the muzzle fall, I would try to have it pointing at a target.

His disadvantage was he couldn't come at me without making a lot of noise. Also, he had chosen to force the issue.

A mistake, because he could have waited for me to freeze or faint.

He tried stealth. Little crunch, little crunch, like a reluctant cereal eater. Silence. I was supposed to forget I'd heard him. Then a scramble. When his head and gun appeared, he was well off to the left and it took him a moment to spot me. I brought the rifle down and fired. He ducked his head and fired several shots without looking, then slid out of sight. But now he had me targeted. On my knees, I shifted a few feet to the other side of my tree.

He came up ten feet further to the left, we traded shots, and he ducked again. Then he decided to let the cold get me. Maybe he had seen my arm. He was silent, and I was silent. Too tired to change positions.

Losing consciousness.

It was a while before I noticed he had left behind his eyeglasses, the rimless ones, which he would need for shooting. One lens was catching the sunlight. They weren't far away, out of reach but close enough that I could see the hole in the other lens.

14

The Suzuki's heater was ferociously efficient.

Half my mind, lulled by the roaring warmth, wanted to shut down for a nap. Most of the rest was paying too much attention to bits of flesh that were awakening—ears, fingers, much of the face, an entire arm, which felt on fire from shoulder to wrist. A useless little clerk was adding and subtracting current damage and further risks and running a ruler down a must-do list. No point in worrying which fleshy parts were actually frostbitten as opposed to just painfully cold. No point in speculating about the wound to the right arm, as long as it wasn't bleeding. The list of business worth attending to had fingerprints at the top. The clerk knew nothing about the security police's forensic talents, had to assume they were competent. On the rifle, I had done my best to wipe away evidence. On Sampson's car, no use trying; I had forgotten all the places I had touched and my blood was all over. If they were any good, I wouldn't be able to pretend I hadn't been part of the show.

I fumbled out my phone. No signal.

So I put the Suzuki in gear, bumped back onto the highway, and drove north.

The young man on duty sounded exactly like Sampson, who had sounded like Butts when he could sound like anyone. "Where are you?" the duty man said.

I told him.

It was Kalocsa, sixty kilometers north of Baja. Still on the north-south highway, but you wouldn't stop unless you wanted to roll around in the locally grown paprika. Innes's friends, if he had any, wouldn't stop. I hoped the logic held. I had found a not very respectable-looking restaurant on a side street, well away from Szabadsag ter, and went in with my coat over my arm and hand. A thousand-forint note got the attention of the woman tending the front. She showed me the telephone but insisted on dialing. I said to hell with security and let her.

"You had better get me a doctor," I said.

A moment later, Glasgow was on the line. "Where are you?"

"A restaurant."

"Can you get out of sight?"

"Does Kalocsa have a hotel?"

"Hold on." Murmuring. "Beta, at Szentharomsag Square. It's a half mile from Szabadsag. Can you get there?"

"I've got a car. Someone else's."

"Is that a problem?"

"It will be."

She made a sound, told me where to park it, she would have it gone in an hour, and for God's sake leave the keys. I told her the make and color and because the very sweet old thing was hanging close to me launched into a vigorous discussion of our dinner plans that mentioned Gambrinus twice and Budapest—*pesht*, so she would understand—three times, with only one glance at my watch. Yes, we would have a fine time tonight. I gave the old woman a frankly lascivious smile, and she backed away.

Glasgow said, "What condition are you in? For the doctor?"

"The bleeding's stopped."

"What about John Sampson?"

I hung up the phone without answering. She was talking to me, wasn't talking to him. What the hell did she think?

So I went outside and they were there, of course, two of them in long blue coats with revolvers holstered on the outside. The

Suzuki had all their attention, and they were displeased. The bigger man's peripheral vision caught me coming out of the restaurant. He whirled, made a snap judgment, and jerked a finger at me and reeled me in. *This car, which I must plainly see, was it mine?*

The mental clerk ran down my options. Shrug, pretend I had never seen it. They looked officious enough to search me, and they would find the key and a bullet wound. Then there was turn and run like the devil. I couldn't sustain a fast walk. The only real choice was to shuffle up and be a friendly American. I had gotten gloves on in the toilet, hadn't had the nerve to run water over the hand but had covered up the evidence. I sketched a left-handed greeting, asked them if something was wrong with my car. Bad luck, one had fair English. The car was illegally parked, that was wrong, and only a few feet from a sign that stated plainly that parking was not allowed. I looked up and down the street. The Suzuki was the only parked vehicle, the only vehicle at all; a third rate side street and they didn't want you parking on it. In Budapest, the side streets were parked two deep. In Kalocsa, they kept order.

"I didn't recognize the restriction."

But the sign was very clear. They consulted and agreed it was. Was it possible I had ignored it?

No, no. I believed visitors should be respectful of a host country's laws (there had to be a couple I hadn't broken in the last few days), especially too of their great institutions such as parking customs.

He raised eyebrows that looked plucked. "Yet you have violated this law, which is necessary to keep the streets clear for the many buses that carry tourists to our splendid craft shops."

I nodded regretfully, felt the ground swirl; I was close to fainting but I had to remember to tell the doctor I didn't want blood, not here, thank you.

Whatever the bigger man read on my face wasn't enough different from the usual scofflaw's pale sweats to interest him.

He shrugged. He was the senior man and he was tired of standing in the cold toying with the American.

"It will be enough this time if you move the car," he said. He arched the eyebrows at his colleague, who concurred.

I stepped around to the driver's side.

And over his shoulder, he asked, "Did you say the vehicle was yours?"

I could make up any name. Avis, Peter Rice. But they could hold me while they checked.

"Mine for the day," I said.

I could volunteer more, but couldn't mention Innes, so I left it at that, *Mine for the day*, as if it were an answer, and I opened the door and they walked away.

Dumb. If they had used a nightstick just a little, I'd have shown them a hell of a crime scene.

I started the engine and sat still, waiting for the patrol to reach the end of the street. It wouldn't do if they saw the pathetic spectacle of a man trying to shift gears and steer with his left hand.

Once I was in second gear, I found I could tool around at most town speeds by riding the clutch, brake and gas in varying combinations. Innes wasn't going to care what I did to his transmission.

15

"Tell me this. How did Innes *know*?" Magdalena Glasgow's beautiful mouth was twisted into a biting shape.

It was a strange question. Not *Why did he try the hit?* but *How did he know you would be on the road?*

"He must have followed us from Budapest," I said.

Jeremy Butts rolled his eyes. "Not damn likely, Sampson missing a tail."

"Or," Glasgow said, "you were looking for a payoff and told Innes."

"Told Innes what? For what payoff?" I was almost too tired to argue. "Anyway, I couldn't have told my mother. Sampson took me straight from the hotel to his car."

They were beginning to annoy me, with their sanctimoniousness and high-mindedness.

"You're not funny." I had been responding to Glasgow, but Jeremy Butts was easier to provoke. He was sitting on the bed in the dimming light. It had taken them a long time to get the embassy doctor on the road. Whatever he'd shot me up with was making me sleepy. Chipped tibia, very ugly exit wound. I'd sat on the toilet with sheets of plastic covering the toilet and the floor, looking hard off to the left while he used the wash basin as an operating table. Standing to the side, Butts held me steady when I fainted. The butcher had shot in anesthetic, so it wasn't the pain—wasn't then—but the bloody smell was too much. Like working behind a meat counter, except they wouldn't let this bastard handle sausage. Too rough on any kind of flesh that came his way. He couldn't resist scissoring off the ragged ends, hoarding them in a pan for the grinder, and —

"Are you going to throw up again?" the doctor had said pleasantly.

I had my eyes closed.

"If you are, I can wait a moment."

The solicitous, caring tone was pure evil. He enjoyed the scissoring and chopping. *Be more practical to take off the arm.*

I swam back into focus. Was losing track of time. Wasn't funny, wasn't I? The gray room was tilted and runny at the edges. Magdalena Glasgow was gone. Jeremy Butts looked hard-faced and businesslike, trying to convince himself they lost an agent every week, this was combat, casualties to be expected, to the greater glory of Ivy League sculling. He hadn't seen Sampson with an exit wound the size of a dinner plate, or Innes, brains sprayed over the snow like gray jelly. Someone else had gotten the cleanup job.

"Your boss seems upset," I said, just to be thinking about something. "Was Sampson her son?" Virgin birth, I nearly added, but it would cast them all in the wrong light.

"We're all her sons."

Couldn't tell how he felt about that. Not Oedipal.

"What the hell *is* this operation?"

"Stitching you up." The butcher. Dr. Slaughter.

"Maggie's operation."

Butts didn't wince. Didn't answer.

The doctor stuck something in my arm, and the room vanished.

"Let's try it again," said a female voice.

"All right."

"Tell me who you talked to this morning."

"Sampson."

"Besides Sampson."

"You."

"Besides me."

"A security officer."

"Yes?"

I didn't know if she meant yes besides him or yes what about. I said, "He took my passport."

"Who else."

"I don't remember."

"Are you trying?"

"No."

"Do your best."

I tried. The room was dark, which helped. Her voice was somewhere close, friendly, confidential, almost intimate, reassuring. If I couldn't, really couldn't remember, she wouldn't be angry. I knew that and wanted very badly to remember. Knew, with equal certainty, that the doctor had stuck something in my arm that made me want to help. Floating vaguely an inch above the bed, I thought the doctor's idea was good, it would help break down inhibitions, make us all closer.

"Isabelle," I said. Isabelle of the blue KLM uniform. We'd talked at breakfast. I explained slowly, afraid the order of the words was incoherent.

"Did you talk about your drive?"

"I didn't know about the drive."

"What then?"

"Springtime in the Netherlands." I had been trying to pick her up. I explained this to the voice.

"What about Innes?"

"What about?"

"When did you talk to him?"

"Didn't."

"You can remember."

"Really didn't." Not today, not once, not even as he slid around on the hard snow and tried to kill me.

"Let's try again," she said.

□□□

"So she said she was a reporter."

Deborah Wolfe.

"Yes, for NPR."

"And she was interested in Gabor?"

I had come out of it enough that the sense of intimacy was gone. So was the urge to help. I was trying not to let their absence show. Butts was somewhere in the room. They would have made plans for me, and I wanted to know what sort.

"All right. Do you feel like going back to sleep?"

"Yes."

"Then go ahead. You deserve a rest." A whisper: "How long?"

"He could be under for five or six hours." The meat cutter. He should have his license yanked.

"Stay with him."

"My wife—"

"We're not going back to Budapest."

"*I* need to go. And I don't have a car."

"The van will pick you up at midnight. Keep him quiet till then."

"Oh, I'll keep him quiet." Bitter and small. He would be quick with the needle. He moved around in the dark after they left. Settled into a chair, turned on a lamp and hissed "Christ!" as something scuttled along a baseboard.

I kept my eyes slitted and fought sleep. He wasn't very good. When he said four or five hours, the patient should be out that long. I wasn't even having to struggle to stay awake.

The bed trembled, rocked a little, mattress no longer soft, spine rattling as the driver shifted into a higher gear. Then it was smooth going, a highway. They'd brought me half awake to walk me out of the hotel. I didn't remember getting into the van. Wondered how long I'd been out.

"Are you feeling better?"

Butts.

I opened my eyes. My stomach was doing jumps, my arm ached, and the back of my head was pounding. How much dope had the butcher given me?

"We're almost there."

I looked around, wondered if they'd used the same van to clean up the accident scene, whether they'd sluiced it out afterward. Butts and I were the only passengers in the back. The van was big enough that the cab and body were separate.

"Almost where?" I said.

He glanced at a watch.

"We're going back to Budapest?"

He didn't answer.

I was sitting up, then. Rocking, nauseated.

"Don't worry," he said. "You're just along for the ride."

"The ride where?"

Silence. Not Budapest.

The toilet at the end of the hall hadn't been cleaned since Brezhnev visited, and he'd had disgusting habits. We were further south, in somebody's idea of a safe house in Baja. I came back to the room with my face damp and cold. Jeremy Butts and another, older man with a three-day beard leaned close to the table, beside which sat Magdalena Glasgow, a tiny phone pressed to her ear. Dr. Slasher's feet showed on the bed in the adjoining room. An unhappy man, he'd gone on strike upon hearing he wouldn't get home tonight.

The woman set the phone down. She talked to the bearded man. "Smetana has been in and out twice since noon."

"Is Preston sure?" he said. He was in his forties, built for heavy work.

"Why are you surprised?"

"I'm surprised they're so clumsy."

"With Innes out of pocket, they don't know if they're blown."

I sat on a corner of the room's double bed. It didn't invite closer contact. The phone beeped, and Glasgow picked it up and listened. Then she said, "Chandler and Preston are inside the gate. Nobody but the watchman is present."

Her tension could be smelled.

Jeremy Butts came around the table, stomach puffed out, hands on top of his head, pretending confidence. "If they get the goods, we go home."

I said, "Then what happens?"

"Then the State Department sends a note about the transiting of weapons into Serbia or wherever. Budapest shuts down this line. Smetana looks for a new way to make trouble." He paced. Neither Glasgow nor the bearded man shut him up. "The wars are going to spread. Hungary is afraid of the Serbs, so they hope the Croats will beat them back. Then they can bitch about the way Croatia treats its ethnic Hungarians. Same beef as they've got against Romania, Slovakia, Czech Republic. All their neighbors."

"And you folks stick your finger in to make it all peaceful."

My arm was aching, but I didn't want another painkiller from Dr. Slasher. He was too angry to be trusted. When the arm hurt, it was hard to think of their operation as diplomacy. I ignored Butts and tried to talk to the woman. "That plant wasn't in condition to produce anything."

"Two rail cars shunted in this morning. They were unloaded before noon." She settled back in the chair but wasn't comfortable. It was after two a.m., and her boys were still out playing.

Forty minutes. The report came. Useless machinery, nothing operable, calling it a night.

16

Twenty thousand dollars.

Four days' work, more or less. I put the check in my billfold, moving stiffly, and thanked Chester Holt.

"I am sorry you have other commitments," Holt said. He tried a simpering smile that no one but a cynic could mistrust. "Have you injured your arm?"

"A car ran me off the road yesterday."

"My word. How did it happen?"

"We were near Baja. A fellow from Marriott is in town looking for resort properties."

"I wouldn't call that a resort area, would you Mrs. Holt?"

"Absolutely unappealing."

"Was your companion injured?"

"No, he drove over to Lake Balaton this morning."

"Did you speak to the other driver?"

I adopted his aphoristic style. "People who run you off the road have a way of not stopping."

"I'm certain. It says something about human character, alas."

The Corvinus's violin players got too close, injecting the squeals of Gypsies leaping over bloodied knives. Charity's mouth snapped shut, and they pulled back.

"Our own venture in Baja is proceeding apace," Holt said. "Yesterday we got two computer-operated lathes and a mile of electrical cable. Moving ahead, moving ahead."

A couple of decrepit lathes and a ton of electrical scrap

hadn't filled two boxcars, but it was all Glasgow's people had found. The trucks that hauled the rest of the shipment away must have come in between dusk and ten p.m., while her boys were busy cleaning up the roadside.

"When will you be in operation?" I said.

"Very soon. It will be on a small scale at first, until we can get the kinks out. Then, who knows? This is where we're going to see capitalism's next giant step. I'm convinced of that, aren't I, Mrs. Holt?"

"Chester takes a bit of convincing, but then it's impossible to change his mind."

"Inertia and momentum in the same head." He chuckled, inviting me to join him. Here we were, the Budapest branch of the Indianapolis Rotary.

I heard the humming before Holt's attention shifted and he said, "Hello, Jimmy!" as the wheelchair rolled up. "Enough work for one day, my boy. This is Patrick McCarry, middleman extraordinaire. What are you drinking?"

"Some of that brandy, Mr. Holt."

"The syrupy stuff?"

"Yes sir."

My peripheral vision couldn't pick up Smetana. Scooping my napkin off the table gave me a chance for a better look. He was on a sofa in the lobby, reading.

"Jim Wilkes is the best engineer east of the Mississippi," Holt said, "which makes Charity wonder why he works for us. Those talents aside, the boy doesn't know his liquor."

The boy was at least early middle-aged. Whatever put him in the wheelchair had drained him. He looked thin and dry, not necessarily weak.

"What kind of engineering do you do?" I said.

"What kind of middlemanning do you do?"

"Financial, mainly."

"Patrick helped us get the factory," Holt said.

"I don't owe him any thanks for that. If that brick pile was any worse, it wouldn't have a roof. That would be a plus. We wouldn't be there."

"Now, Patrick didn't choose the spot. Your boss did. The price was right. The problems can be fixed." As the drinks arrived, Chester Holt looked at me. "What is your next project, Patrick? Resort properties? Or back to London?" Silent laughter was threatening to erupt. Wilkes didn't seem to get it. But Mrs. Holt cracked half a smile. They were a jolly old pair.

I stopped at the concierge's desk, signed the check to Paribas, dropped it in a DHL envelope. As long as Hruby had the passport, I couldn't get myself out of the country. But the check could travel. Check, not money. It would become money if it cleared Holt Industries' Indianapolis bank.

Chester could have several reasons for bouncing a check on me. Why pay a dead man? I was assuming that he'd had something to do with Innes's excursion. If anyone in town didn't know I was canoodling with the CIA, they must have been dumb and blind.

A voice near my shoulder said, "Is that your client—Mr. Holt—in the bar?"

So she'd done some homework but not enough. If she had known what she was doing, they would have looked to her like a tableful of happy jackals.

"Deborah Wolfe," she reminded me.

"Why don't you have a drink with me," I said, "and forget Mr. Holt."

"I might do the drink, but first I want to meet your client."

I couldn't tell her he was dangerous. I had known enough reporters to know a hint of corruption would be like firing her from a catapult. *Oh, Mr. Holt, is it true your Belgian company makes machine guns and you kill people. I'm from NPR, tell me all about yourself,* as if the press card doubled as a magic charm. As if it promised, *You can't kill me, I'm a reporter.*

I wouldn't get away with another version: Mr. Holt can't talk, delicate negotiations, maybe in six weeks. What reporter minded getting in the way of negotiations?

I went back into the bar with her, a step behind as she closed on the Holts' table.

"Hi, Mr. Holt, I'm Deborah Wolfe. Here's my card. I'd sure like to interview you for the radio." She hovered over him, wide smile, perky hair, as back-home as a cookout on the Wabash.

"I told her you're too busy," I said. Hoping he understood: No need to send a shooter.

"Well, now" — he took her wrist in a stubby hand — "do I look too busy? Pull up a chair for the lady, McCarry. So you do radio stories. Where you from, sweetheart?"

"Waukegan."

"That's like next door. We're from Indianapolis. This is my darling wife Charity, and my engineer Jim Wilkes." He dug out a business card for her. "What would you like to drink, young lady? I trust you're close to twenty-one."

She made a pigeon-like noise and would have patted his head if her hand were free. She switched on the tape recorder and went through the routine. Was this a sensible place to do business? Could you rely on a contract? Were the courts honest? He made the diplomatic noises to be expected of a businessman who didn't want to be shut down. Hungarians were pretty reasonable people, Westernized, economically advanced, good partners.

"Will it be possible to export from here?"

"Look at a map, dear. There are good markets in the former Yugoslavia, in Albania, in the Baltic Republics. We've already got sales representatives in the Ukraine and Lithuania. This is just a pilot plant, you understand. But if it's successful, we'll be well positioned for the export market. I can foresee years of expansion."

"There are elections in a few months. Will that affect things?"

"I prefer to stay out of politics."

"I suppose if a right wing government came to power, it would be good for business?"

He made a delicate cutting motion, and she switched off. He beamed at her. "You don't want to get me in trouble, do you?"

"Off the record then?"

"We haven't had a problem with the current government. We'd expect to get along if someone replaces them. Everybody wants economic progress and knows it comes from the private sector. That's especially important when things are depressed."

"What about corruption?"

"It may be a problem elsewhere in Europe, but I haven't encountered it here. We can put that on the record, if you'd like."

She would, they did, and when she noticed nobody at the table was saying much, she finished her drink. We wandered through the lobby. I felt uneasy, like a rabbit that had run out of lucky feet.

Wolfe said, "I tried reaching Mr. Innes this afternoon, one more shot at Gabor, and the office said they're both out of town." She switched tacks. "Do you think Gabor was a dissident?"

"What?"

"His bio says he got out in fifty-seven. That was the year after the popular uprising. There were a lot of people in prison. Had Nagy been executed then?"

She noted my blank stare, pressed on. "*Imre* Nagy, the prime minister who supported the popular uprising. The Russians hauled him off to Romania and shot him."

It was news to me, quite old news, but still news. I said, "You've been reading up."

She shook her head. "Daddy in Waukegan was a professor of history. I learned about Nagy at his knee."

"Ah. My father taught me how to throw a baseball."

"I've got time for a drink if you want. Tape recorder off."

My shoulders twitched as we stepped outside. I had lost track of Erik Smetana. No shooters, I reminded myself, no need for them. Innes had had a go at our car—here was a plausible explanation—only because nobody wanted visitors while the boxcars were being unloaded. So keep your nose out of it, and there's no need for shooters.

I looked back as the taxi took us to a nightspot Wolfe had chosen called Zoldseg-Gyumoles. The streets were full, and anybody could have been tagging along. We both got out on the curb side. Kiraly utca wasn't busy, but a Mercedes and an Opel were struggling to hold straight courses along the ice ruts. I watched the cars' windows, which stayed rolled up, and followed her inside.

We were too early for the music that drew the younger crowd. Wolfe spotted someone at a table, and when heads bobbed out of the way I saw she was looking at Peter Rice. He wasn't drinking alone. His buddy Andras Kajdi of *People's Voice* sat hunched with his phone against his ear, and another man had his back to us. She pushed her way over and planted a kiss on Peter. "Deborah dear," he said.

"Thanks for the leads. Look who I picked up."

"He's scruffy looking. Join us?"

I pulled over two chairs, one at a time, and we crowded in so that no one was really close to the table. Peter made introductions. The man we'd come up behind had white hair and a long ascetic face. "Jacob Folkestone," Peter said, "of the British League of Journalists. Patrick's a Yank, Jacob, but he's not with the CIA."

Not this evening. Jacob looked doubtful.

"Jacob exposed this hack O'Beollain just the other day on television. 'I think you're from Langley,'" Peter intoned. "Jolly good show, Jacob."

"I'm a Yank, too," Wolfe said.

"You're above suspicion, my dear. We were worrying about the election," Peter said. "It's all Kajdi talks about. He foresees concentration camps, yellow arm bands for the Hebrews. The poll this morning said the Socialists will retain a clear majority with luck."

"If the CIA permits it," Kajdi said.

"Are we certain on whose behalf they'd intervene?" Peter said.

As the responses burst across the table, he rolled his eyes and unwrapped a cigar. "So easy," he whispered to me. "So, you've bought a new topcoat but not leather, and you look as though you're in pain."

"I thought you were on the road."

"Back two hours ago. There's a better story here." A girl wandered close and he held up five fingers. "*Sor.*"

"What sort of story?"

He eavesdropped on the others until the beers arrived. Then he raised a bottle. "Cheers. What would you make of it, Patrick, if I told you the security police were going through the Europa Foundation's offices this afternoon?"

Innes's car must have turned up. I said, "I wouldn't know what to make of it. What do you know about Gabor's assistant, an Englishman named Innes?"

"He's Hungarian, not English."

"I've met him. He's as English as plum pudding."

"You're a sucker for an accent, mate. Innes came to England as a boy, family got out sometime after the revolution. Did Deborah manage to interview Innes?"

"Deborah did but essentially got the brushoff," she said. She'd been talking to Andras Kajdi.

"Pity. God is unreachable, and the first priest won't chat. I tried once as well, Sunday feature in mind, how did Tamás Gabor make all that money? Most of the clods from the Sorbonne and the London School never accomplish much, do they, except for steering African dictators. But then, the average twit who goes to work in the City doesn't build up a billion quid starting from scratch. He gets to be chief trader somewhere or if he'd got connections deputy chairman of his uncle's bank. I would like to know Tamás's trading secrets. Now there would be a book! *How the Average Bloke Can Trade Like Tamás Gabor, as told to Peter Rice.*"

I said, "If the ideas are worth anything, you'd make more using them."

"Don't have the starting capital," Peter said. "Besides, what Gabor could do, you and I can't, even if we sit at his knee. Watching somebody doesn't *make* you that person."

He and Folkestone decided to shove off. I listened as Andras Kajdi shared his alarm with Wolfe. His phone interrupted twice. After the second call, he confided, "I've got an assistant watching the Parliament. It's possible some renegade army faction will join the fascists."

"Is that happening?" she asked.

"It is what I expect." His tone was confident.

I leaned forward because someone had put loud music on, and a few people were groping on the dance floor. I asked Kajdi, "You wrote a story saying Sipos worked for the secret police. How good was your source?"

When he was offended, his English became less Americanized. "I know it is true or I would not have published."

"Was your source in the government?"

He made a brushing-away motion. "I cannot say, of course. But the number of people who would have such information is limited."

"If Sipos informed, who would want him dead?"

He shrugged. "Naturally, the fascists."

Naturally.

He told Wolfe, "It is a revelation when an American sees how this place really works. I'll bet you didn't realize, until you read my report, that we still have the secret police. But it exists today to protect democracy."

"Who runs them?" she asked.

"There are two agencies. One is our Office for Constitutional Protection, in the Interior Ministry, the other is the National Security Office—we say *Nemzetbiztonsagi Hivatal*—which functions under the Prime Minister's direction. Both are much different from the old days." He sized her up and asked, "Are you in Budapest for long?" The phone beeped. He listened, snapped something in Magyar. When he shut the phone, he stared between us as if he'd lost his train of thought.

Wolfe said, "Do you think I could interview your man at the Parliament?"

That brought him back to thinking about her. He smiled quickly. "It would have to be off the record."

She sighed. "I'm used to that."

I walked into my hotel room and found them there, watching a dirty movie off German satellite. There were two of them, both in uniform, which consisted of charcoal suits, cap toe shoes, white shirts, sedate ties. I hadn't met either before. I wondered how big a stable Magdalena Glasgow kept.

A Burly Burgers card came out. The blond man said, "She wants to see you."

"Usual terms, a needle in the arm and soft music?"

"I think it's your chance to leave the country, if you want to."

17

We sat in the backseat of a Mercedes, and she handed me the passport. The name was the right one — I held the page down, getting pretty good one-handed, as I checked — and the face was familiar. Stamps in order. *MK-Ferihegy I.* in magenta, Gatwick in gray. Fine. Nothing in a language I could decipher that said ARREST THIS MAN. I wrapped my billfold around it.

"Tell Captain Hruby thanks."

She said nothing. The silent distaste was supposed to shame me into telling her something I had been holding back.

I said, "The government's security police apparently visited the Europa Foundation."

"That's not what I'm interested in."

I understood why. If Gabor was involved in whatever had set Innes off, it wouldn't be something as small-time as running guns down to Serbia. Besides which, did she really believe Serbia needed guns?

"You and the Hungarians should work together," I said.

"That's out of the question."

I took a turn at the silence game. She held out for a half minute, then said, "I'm interested *only* in keeping an American citizen from causing trouble."

"If you mean me, I'm happy not to cause trouble. But I wonder, what put the security police onto the Europa Foundation? Unless Innes has turned up?"

"You can forget about that." She shrugged. "The

foundation called them in. They have an important missing person."

"The secret police handle missing persons?"

"For Mr. Gabor. Now, tell me about Holt."

"The engineer, Wilkes, doesn't like the factory. There was no hint of a destination for whatever they brought in. The Holts were happy with themselves."

"Smetana?"

"Sticking close." It was all stuff her own people must have reported, not worth liberating my passport over, but I wasn't giving it back. I sat and waited. Traffic zipped along Terez korut. We sat against the curb, engine and heater running. The middle-aged man who had been in Baja was the driver. The morning was overcast and cold. The traffic didn't have to ride along ruts because Terez was a major street and the snow had been plowed into five-foot-high reefs along the curbs and in the median.

I told myself I didn't hold a grudge over the needle. "There's a reporter who had the Parliament staked out last night," I said. "He was waiting for something."

She ignored me.

I said, "Has Smetana gotten a shipment across the border?"

"No."

So she had the border monitored. I hoped it was Butts, sitting with long lenses to his face as his feet froze.

I said, "If Holt has brought guns in, perhaps they're meant to stay here; to be used here."

She said, "I don't credit talk of a coup. Every café intellectual has the same story."

Andras to a T, I thought. "But it would be messy if an American like Holt were involved in one."

A car had been sitting behind us for too long. I could see the black snout and tinted windshield when I looked at Glasgow. She may not have been aware of it; her driver hadn't said anything. I wondered if I should mention it.

"There's no way a coup could succeed, could it Carl?"

"You've got ten million people in Hungary," the driver said, "and nine and a half million, maybe nine and three quarters, managed to coexist with the Communists. Six or seven million of them are nostalgic for the old days when their jobs were safe."

"Scratch your idea, McCarry." She settled back, wrapped in a moth-eaten fur.

A light changed, and as a tide of zigging cars bore up the avenue, Carl slipped the gear lever and moved into the center lane ahead of the traffic. The car that had been behind us followed.

"Do you plan to leave town right away or pack your bags first?" Glasgow said.

"Am I free to leave?"

"You're of no use to us. Unless you can stay close to Chester Holt."

"The job is finished."

"What did he pay you? Half a civil servant's annual salary?" Her dislike filled the car, she couldn't help it.

"He paid me more than the job was worth, which was about five cents," I said.

They dropped me at the next corner. I flagged a taxi and headed for the hotel before thinking to look. The tinted windshield was three cars back, trying to hide behind a delivery van. I didn't like that. If someone was more interested in me than in Glasgow's team, it meant they thought I was a player. They didn't understand that once I had taken Holt's check and kissed his hand, I meant to be out of it.

I gave the taxi driver a new address. No. 2 József Attila utca. We would see if they really wanted to play. The dark snout and tinted windshield peeled off a block before we reached the Interior Ministry headquarters. That didn't tell me much. They didn't want to play in this neighborhood—or they were right at home and didn't want me knowing.

We got back on the Outer Ring Road. It was tricky because the ring's name changed every few blocks. We crossed Kossuth

Rakoczi utca, and the next segment because Erzsebet korut. The neighborhood was heavily commercial and busy, with streetcars, buses and delivery trucks trying to occupy the same space as darting passenger cars. Pedestrians didn't dare cross except through underground passages.

Then the avenue forked, and I slapped the seat back and pointed to the curb. I gave him about twice the meter, bounded out within ten feet of the entrance to an underpass.

They'd picked us up again coming off a side street, not even discreet about it. The car was a snappy new Lada, straight from Russia, only decent thing made in the East, according to Peter. They were two cars back because they hadn't been able to force themselves into traffic right away.

As I left the cab, they tried slowing right behind us, but a truck had obscured our move for too long and they couldn't get in front of it. The best they could have done was to pull parallel to us, with a lane separating, stand on the brake and unload.

Instead they worked their way to the curb six or eight car lengths ahead. I was on the steps into the underpass as the passenger sprang out. Choppy impression: brown jacket, blue jeans, driving cap, nothing about the face except it was clean-shaven.

I went straight down, crossed to the farthest wall of the shopping arcade, and watched the stairway. Much depended on how many people they had. Because of the road's fork, the underpass had four exits, two down rather long passages. I stayed put and waited and the driving cap didn't follow. *Couldn't*, I realized. I could take any of the ways out, to different sides of the streets, and if he was underground he wouldn't know which one I had chosen. So he and probably his driver were standing on tiptoes waiting for me to emerge. I took in the surroundings: a half dozen shops, stemware, Fuji film, shoes, plenty of people, which was bad because I hadn't got a look at the driver. He could come right up and put an arm on me, or even things up for Innes, and unless brown jackets and jeans were the uniform of the day, I wouldn't see him coming. I couldn't stay here long anyway. With a radio or a phone, if they had the manpower they could cover the area.

Once they had plugged the holes, they could come down into the burrow to pull out the rabbit.

I emerged on a side street. A policeman was arguing with a man I took to be the driver of the car, and driving cap was standing over the nearest hole, glaring at me from two streets away. To resume the chase, he would have to ditch the cop, drive against five lanes of traffic, overcome two steel rail barricades, and scare a few dozen pedestrians out of the way.

It bothered me the cop was still giving the driver hell.

It meant they weren't Hruby's or the P.M.'s men.

I told the taxi driver to keep going past the hotel. It was the second time. I was an amateur at the game, but there was no question that the black SUV on the other side of the road had occupants.

I sat far back in the seat, longing for the straightforward duplicity of Wall Street.

My driver had stopped. He raised both hands, lifting the invisible burden of ignorance. He had run out of instructions. Where did I wish to go?

I told him.

"They could be plain clothes security," Jeremy Butts said. We were in the shabby building where I had first met Glasgow. The office still looked like it was on loan. The window rattled as a truck went up the street.

"They'd have flashed a badge at the traffic cop in that case," I said.

"Could be Smetana's people. He'd have men in the field." Jeremy Butts set a pair of fancy Zeiss binoculars on his knee. When anyone was on the street, he had the sense not to use them. He was looking at parked cars, trying to see whether there was anything behind the windshields.

I sank into my coat.

"There are a few reporters in town," I said, "who think something's going on. My next phone calls are to several of them. Good material—why are a gun broker's people staking out such and such addresses. Why's an American embassy car with a certain tag number"—I recited his BMW's—"hauling Burly Burgers employees? Then an interview with an American financial adviser who has a bullet wound with messy surgery. Colorful."

"You can't bluff us."

"No?"

"Your story isn't worth much once we describe your SEC trouble."

"Even if I'm a liar, a reporter might decide the embassy is tampering with the election. That could get you all thrown out."

"You're assuming we don't liaise with the locals."

He hadn't been there when his boss called that impossible. I said, "You and Maggie must wonder about the locals. The country is crawling with informers. Yet somehow Holt has managed to set up a weapons depot right under the government's noses. What do you do if Hungary *wants* arms shipped south?"

"Not much," he said, but I could read the next silence. If the Hungarian government knew, it owed his agency for Sampson.

I brought him back to my problem. I wanted Butts to believe that my trouble was his trouble and give me cover.

"Do you *have* to get to your hotel?" he demanded. "I could drive you straight to the airport."

"I've got papers at the hotel, and a couple of handpainted neckties."

He sighed, walked to a cabinet and made a show of drawing out a small pistol with a black holster.

"Let's have a look," he said.

18

He put me out of the car, and I sprinted between parked vans. He curled left and sat with his tail sticking out, so the SUV would come around the previous corner and pick him up. By the time they skidded into the intersection, Jeremy Butts was two-thirds of a block down. They clipped a fender making the turn and creased a van overcorrecting.

He was making no promises on how long I had. Nor that we hadn't missed a second stakeout after luring this group away from the hotel. "It's not as if you're worth all that much manpower," he said, never taking his eyes off the street. "These clowns are so bad they must be from Kelly Girls. Strictly amateurs. Bail out now."

I was operating one and a quarter-handed. No nerve damage, Dr. Slaughter had murmured, disappointed he couldn't take the arm. *Might develop infection*—he'd sounded more hopeful. I could hold things that weren't heavy; could raise the elbow a foot away from my side. It took me five minutes, when I got back to the hotel, to pack what I wanted and switch off the light. I took an elevator down as far down as the skyway, which would connect to the other side of the street.

Two people were coming along the balcony overlooking the lobby.

Andras Kajdi saw me and gave a solemn nod. Deborah Wolfe was traveling light, no recorder hanging outside the heavy skin jacket. She pulled off a knit cap. "We were looking mainly for Peter," she said. "Andras is interested in your clients."

He wore a canny squint. "This is for a possibly political article."

"You've said the magic word. I'm late for an appointment."

"Last night, Deborah and I put our heads together. Most interesting."

She covered a blush with a smile.

I was holding my suitcase in my left hand, and it was getting heavy.

"Deborah had part of a story, you see, and without knowing it I had the other part. My sources had told me there were two men in the country on a mission threatening the security of our democracy. An Erik Smetana—that was a name I was familiar with. And a James Wilkes, from a Belgian company, TACEM. And whom does Deborah meet while interviewing Mr. Holt?"

"Jim Wilkes," she said. "Remember?"

I remembered.

"He works for Mr. Holt," she said.

I told Andras, "Your sources are always coming up with something exotic. Sipos was working for the secret police."

"The security authorities, the Office for Constitutional Protection."

"To me, it looked like he was pimping for the stripper bars. Now the Holts tie in to people threatening your democracy." I glanced at the woman, hoping to steer their professional interests apart. "It sounds as though all Andras's fantasies are converging."

It didn't work. She leaned toward Kajdi, deciding to distrust me.

"The piece of information you may be missing," he said, "or may not is that TACEM manufactures arms and munitions. Another piece of information that Deborah had, which I did not, fills in the picture. Holt has arranged some kind of business with Tamás Gabor. He's a financier."

"I know who Gabor is."

"Of course. You work with the Holts."

His implication was pretty clear. I'd worked with Holt. Holt had a connection with TACEM, which made guns. I had a connection with TACEM, with guns.

"How do the pieces fit?" I said, more to the woman.

"Andras thinks Gabor may be bankrolling the far right."

"My sources," he said—and the phrase scraped my nerves— "say your people have a warehouse down south. The town is called Baja."

Deborah nodded him on. "Patrick didn't want me interviewing Mr. Holt," she said.

They were giving me narrow looks.

"If I had to write my article right now," Kajdi said, "there would be a big coincidence I couldn't explain. We've got these intruders—TACEM, Wilkes, Smetana, Holt—and over here somewhere we've got the wealthiest man in Hungary, and right in between there's this American dude nobody in town knows, supposedly an investment adviser but he flies in from London instead of New York, starts trying to get Holt in tight with Gabor's people—you're surprised I know?—hires a local hustler, who having fulfilled his usefulness is found assassinated. Who do we suppose this American is working for? Isn't the most likely answer the CIA?" He splayed his fingers, gave a little shrug. "That is what I would write today."

He hadn't found out about my fling with Maggie or he wouldn't be asking. I said, "Great work."

"A reporter with all those facts has a story," Andras said, "but not necessarily the right story."

"Don't let that stop you."

I brushed past them.

He tagged along. "You know, we are all paranoid. We had the Kinder Gentler Brothers operating here for so long, pretty much running the AVO—that was the old secret police—and now we've all got the CIA on our minds."

Wolfe was right behind me. "I don't know what's got you so upset. It's not that we really think you're with—"

I halted. "Why don't you shout it from the balcony?"

She lowered her voice. "I mean"—lowered it again—"you run around a lot, and nobody seems to know why, all mysterious, hang out with cripples in the arms industry—did you know he got himself blown up, by the way?—so it's—"

"What?"

"That's why he's in a wheelchair. What did you think I meant?" She squinted, didn't see an answer. "What we were planning to do," she said, "is play tag with Holt's people, see if they head down to their warehouse. See?—I wouldn't have told you that if we thought you really were with the CIA. Would I, Andras?"

I could have been wearing a station chief's beanie and they wouldn't have got it.

"If you're at all close to right about the warehouse," I said, "your scheme is dangerous."

"I've had experience," Andras said.

"Was it your AVO friends who told you about the warehouse?" They had to know, KGB training and all.

"The AVO has been disbanded, I told you. We now have—"

"—an Office for Constitutional Protection and a National Security Office. And none of the old comrades have stayed on, right?"

"A good reporter has sources, not friends, in government." He squared himself up. "If you'd seen my play—'The Boot'— you would understand I'm no buddy of secret policemen."

I let it pass. "What does the warehouse matter? Do you think it's storing bazookas?"

"And grenade launchers, and mortars. It's a good bet."

I didn't want them on my conscience. If Peter were around, he would have talked sense, said people *running* guns probably believe in *using* guns, and anyway, Deborah dear, you wouldn't do anything so stupid in Harlem or Brooklyn, so why in Budapest?

If I tried, it would be CIA smoke, promptly rejected. She was hot for a story. Andras was hot to impress her. Just the team to tail Erik Smetana.

"Of course, you could come with us," she said.

No, I don't think so. *Sipos, Sampson, Innes. Dr. Slaughter's magic needle.*

I spoke to Andras, "What makes you so damned sure that's how the pieces add up—TACEM, Holt, Smetana, Gabor, warehouse, grenades?"

"I'm not damned sure." He was easily wounded today. "It's a plausible hypothesis."

We had walked as we argued, gotten past the early prostitutes on the skyway. The street below looked clear.

I stopped. "You've got experience, have you?"

"A journalist—"

Cripes.

"Have you got a car?"

"Of course."

"Go scout the street, see if we've got anybody watching at either end. Then you can give me a ride."

He handed me his phone and I punched in the number.

"I'm looking for Jeremy."

"Yeah . . . ?" A flat American voice, used to working in a shoe store that never had the right size.

"This is McCarry."

"Oh." He gave it a one-two-three pause. "That's not a name we know."

Clicked off.

I handed Andras his phone. So much for recruiting armed backup.

"Who's Jeremy?" Wolfe said.

"An information officer at the embassy. He could give you official help."

"I don't take official help."

Independent press, couldn't be compromised.

I didn't want them blown off the road. Didn't want to drop in on whatever was going on at Holt's factory. I wondered if we could drive round in circles till I spotted a suitably grimy empty building far from the action.

"I have it," Andras announced. He had been phoning off and on, gabbing in Magyar, while the woman drove the rented Panda through side streets. "I've obtained the exact location."

"Who gave it to you?"

His look was pitying. He would never say.

"If it's somebody who knows," I said, "you should wonder how they know."

"This is Budapest. Everybody knows something. Want us to drop you?"

I didn't want to be around when they got themselves killed. "Any corner."

Wolfe nodded understanding.

Telling them would do no good. They knew nobody would mess with *two* reporters on a mission.

I said, "If you're going to do something stupid, after dark would be better. If self-preservation matters to you."

Wolfe took her eyes off the road just long enough to look at me in the mirror. She asked how I knew, and I couldn't just say I *knew*. So to hell with Glasgow's secrets.

"Gabor's assistant bushwhacked us on the highway. He and a CIA agent got onto a fatal shootout."

"You mean Mr. Innes?"

"And a Mr. Sampson."

"My God," she said. "The CIA *is* involved?"

She and Andras traded glances. He opened his phone and she grabbed his hand. "No, no, baby. We both file this one at the same time."

19

There was nothing to do but kill us.

Andras understood. Deborah Wolfe was still thinking about interviews, but Andras had the decency to keep his thought to himself. They couldn't turn us loose. They couldn't keep us in a cellar for two or three months.

She didn't understand. "This is your chance to tell the world."

The grizzled man to whom she had offered that opportunity closed the door and there was nothing but the smell. The truck they had put us in had spent most of its life transporting hogs.

"Shit," Wolfe said. "Do you think he understood?"

"His English wasn't good," Andras said. "Give them a little while. The advantages of getting the truth out will become apparent to their leaders."

He did a good job of sounding convinced.

"I guess they don't heat this thing," she said.

They shuffled in the dark, huddling for warmth. Lacking stomach for an execution, our captors might just leave us here and let the cold to do the job. But I didn't think these people could afford to have weak stomachs. Even the mild-faced older man in the corduroy coat, who had locked us in here, would lift his gaze to sight a gun. *Sending regrets.* I had overheard the phrase while Glasgow's doctor poked me and somebody else—Carl?—talked in the background. You sent regrets when somebody died.

While the door was open, I had taken a fast look around and hadn't seen anything useful in the cargo box. The space was six or seven feet by fifteen, a self-contained enclosure attached to a scabrous cab. There wasn't even a ramp aboard for getting the live cargo in and out. We'd had to hoist ourselves using a strap inside the door. The doors were old-fashioned, with an external locking bar and gravity latch. They could leave us here forever and we couldn't do anything about it.

I paced off the area. Hard to do in the dark, one hand brushing the wall, but it didn't take long. I hadn't seen anything on the walls, and my hand didn't find anything.

Andras said, "We're sitting here. Don't walk on us."

"Try not."

"You know, McCarry, there are only four of them."

"What have you got in mind?"

"If one of them comes for us, we could take him, you and I."

We couldn't if he was armed, but Kajdi was talking to make the woman feel better, maybe himself as well, and I thought I might as well sign on. Wishful thinking was better than no thinking. I said, "We could do that."

"I will give the signal."

"Fine."

"We must not allow these fascists to succeed."

"Andras—until we're loose, stop calling them fascists. They're freedom fighters. You want their story." Even if the story went straight to Captain Hruby's office before the *People's Voice*.

Four men, and I hadn't recognized any of them. Three wore city clothes—long cloth or leather coats, fur hats, suits, ties—and were in their thirties or forties. The other was our mild countryman, possibly owner of the truck, who looked older. Two of the city men spoke passable English.

We had driven as far as Kalocsa and waited for dusk, then started the run down to Baja. There were lots of cars and trucks going both directions. That made it impossible to single out a vehicle for concern, so we worried about all of them. We picked up the bridge traffic coming across the Danube into Baja, peeled off from the flow and lingered on the side streets. After a few minutes, Andras was satisfied we didn't have a tail. But anyone who was interested would know where we were going and could be waiting.

He had taken the news on Innes seriously. "It is obviously a protected site," he said. So the idea was to get close, find a place where we could set up and see what traffic was going in and out. No direct contact. We wouldn't drive in and flash press passes and ask for interviews. They had actually been thinking that way.

Andras Kajdi got up, I could hear the truck creak, and began stomping around in the dark.

Wolfe moved close to me. "I hope they don't leave us here."

I was hoping they would. I had been thinking. "Where are your press credentials?"

"In my jacket."

"And your passport?"

"Yes, why?"

Andras had come over. I could feel the air move nearby.

"Give me your papers," I said. I already had my passport out, was digging for the driver's license in the dark, but it felt a lot like credit cards. So I said the heck with it, left the passport wrapped in the full billfold, and stuffed the cash in a pocket. If they found Wolfe's car and went through it, there was plenty of paperwork in my suitcase to identify someone named McCarry. But that didn't have to be me, and even if they got that far, making sense of the unfamiliar stuff would take time. A passport or press i.d. was self-explanatory.

"They're going to be anxious about us," I said. They should have searched us by now, hadn't because we had shocked them badly. For a while the organizational synapses were shorted out. They had patrolled the roads and the plant, but they hadn't expected to *find* a car staking the place out.

I took my papers and groped in the dark. The metal framing ribs were doubled around the doors, with vertical as well as horizontal struts. The interstices created pockets that to the touch were about an inch deep. Jammed in sideways, my billfold stayed in place. I used up two more ribs with the rest of my papers. If they searched with a flashlight, it wouldn't work for two minutes. But they wouldn't be sure we hadn't left our identification in the car.

"But we want them to know we're reporters," Deborah Wolfe said.

"No," I said. "Once they know who we are, they'll know what they have to deal with, and that will tell them how to do it. If we keep them in suspense, it could take them longer to decide. For all they know, we might be CIA, here to help the cause. They won't be sure." Not more than a hundred ten percent, I thought.

Andras refused to give up his papers. "*You* can be CIA, I'll be a journalist."

"Me, too," Deborah said.

Great. Make it easy for them to kill you.

I told the clean-shaven man with the tall black hair, "Miss Glasgow isn't going to like this. You'd better give us back our car keys."

He wasn't impressed. Two sets of journalist credentials spread on the wood table; the table was the only furniture, they hadn't even brought in chairs or a coffee warmer. I wondered what had become of the plant's old caretaker . . . Mihaly Mester, and my teeth rattled because I was standing in my underwear, barefoot on the concrete floor while the other English speaker went through my clothes. He gave up and the man with tall black hair gestured that I could get dressed. He had an intelligent face that would have been roughly handsome except for a crescent scar that descended from the corner of his left eye, under the nose, to the further nostril. At some point a large part of the face had been sliced open. When I had one leg in my trousers, he said, "What happened to your arm?"

He would know already. His friend had inspected the bandage, but I had to keep up appearances. If he watched movies, he would expect a CIA agent to laugh off bullet wounds. I said, "Love bite."

"From Miss Wolfe?"

"No."

"Miss. . . ?"

"Glasgow."

"Indeed?"

"We're attached to the embassy."

"You say we."

I shrugged.

"Which embassy?"

"United States."

"And Miss Wolfe, is she attached to the embassy?"

"No way," Deborah said. "I work for NPR—you know the name? National Public Radio?"

"It is an excellent cover, I am sure."

"I don't need a cover."

He turned back to me. "What does Miss Wolfe do at the embassy?"

"I can't discuss that."

She threw me a look of pure murder. "You lying son—"

"It's classified."

"No it *isn't*. I don't work for the goddamn CIA and *he* does!"

So much for solidarity among captives, but it was all the tribute I could have asked. The truth wouldn't get us anywhere. An artful lie wouldn't. But confusion might keep the clock running.

He looked me over. How many CIA agents he had seen I had no idea. Maybe like Folkestone he saw them everywhere. If he had ever met Butts or Sampson, he wouldn't waste time wondering if I could kill with my bare hands. He picked up the papers, walked around the table, handed them to Wolfe and Kajdi. He towered over the two of them.

"Perhaps it doesn't matter who you are with," he said. "It may suffice if I know why you are here. Are you looking for something?"

Twenty feet behind him were stacked a few dozen wood crates, each longer than it was wide or high, well sized for shipping baseball bats.

I said, "We were looking for a hotel. Got off the main road."

"If you would prefer, you may answer questions without your clothes on."

Andras felt bold. "We're looking for fascist plotters, and we've found them."

"Oh, yes." The man had a very long mouth that knew how to smile. "You write for *People's Voice*. I've seen your reports quite often. I've even attended a performance of one of your plays, in Budapest. Your opposition to fascism is well established."

Andras said, "Thank you."

"If this were nineteen forty-four, it might even be heroic." He turned away from the smaller man, considered Deborah Wolfe, grimaced, turned on me. "I think these two are idiots and you are the problem."

I didn't disagree. They were idiots.

"So you and I will talk." He crooked a finger at the man in country clothes, gave orders in Magyar. The older man hustled the two reporters out. I watched Wolfe's shoulders sag, felt only a little sorry for her. It wasn't much colder in the truck than in here. Maybe next time they would hide their papers.

"So. We will introduce ourselves. My name is József Cseve. What is yours?"

I stared at my feet.

"Don't you wish to remain in your clothes?"

I was cold *in* them.

"Or—do you wish me to ask the woman?"

I watched him under my eyebrows. One of the other city

slickers—the one with English—had gone out with the reporters. That left me with József Cseve and a hulking man in a long coat who seemed to understand nothing that was said. I assumed they both had guns. I assumed the guns would be out before I could reach Cseve.

He read my expression and said, "You have a chivalrous instinct. In my experience, that is rare among people in the intelligence services. You may be a man I can talk to."

Pretty soon, he would ask for specifics on our operation. I couldn't just *tell* him, because Maggie Glasgow's agents would be made of sterner stuff. They would be expected to rush a gun, gnaw a power cord, stick a tongue in a lamp socket. The most cowardly among them would lose a few teeth before babbling.

He looked at the ceiling—man with a sense of theater, the scar helped. He counted the sleeping bats or whatever, and before he got to naming them closed his eyes and asked one word:

"Why?"

Here we were. I could pretend to misunderstand. But Cseve meant:

Why this operation?

I shivered, anticipating the loss of clothes. The funny thing was, even if they froze me and pulled out a fingernail or mashed a testicle or whatever interrogators do—even if I made a good show of resistance—I still couldn't tell them. I had just realized that, and it was like looking down and seeing nothing underfoot, absolutely nothing. Because even if they bought the story I told, as soon as they had wrung me dry there would be a bullet.

If they thought they had the story, a bullet. If they thought they wouldn't get the story—or wouldn't get it soon enough—a bullet. I had to keep Cseve expecting, without delivering. The technique of the prom queen saving it for marriage, or for a pre-med student.

"They don't tell me everything at Bajza"—nice touch, I

thought—"but you must have made a mistake, caught someone's attention."

"You will have to be more informative."

"I don't know why they opened a book." That sounded good, too, a lot more like agency-yak than saying we'd opened a file.

Two shots.

Distinctly individual, spaced about a second apart.

Neither Cseve nor the other man paid any attention.

Not loud, coming through the factory walls, but close.

Neither man pulled a gun. Neither ran to investigate. So the shots were expected.

Cseve noticed I was listening, though there was nothing more to hear. "Go on," he said.

He thought I was stupid, so he made it clear. "Now you must understand I am serious."

I launched myself at him. We were less than twenty feet apart, and he wasn't expecting it. The gun was coming out, but he was going to be too late, maybe I could get to his eyes or tear the flap of face loose along the scar. I didn't expect to be effective, and I didn't expect the leather coat behind me to stand passive. He would have a gun. But all I was after was one eye, or a flap of face, and I was covering the distance as Cseve's hand came up. The fellow behind was taking his time. I wouldn't hear his shots, might not feel them. I would see the flash from Cseve's hand, but even that hadn't happened yet. It was too late and I was on him.

"What about the book?"

Back to business, except that I was on the floor.

"Is your agency working with the Nemzetbiztonsagi Hivatal?"

I looked away. He was paying no attention to the cut on his lip. It was the best I had been able to do. Had tried, lacked experience and half an arm. The numbness was leaving my face. A broken nose, it felt like. The man's image swam.

The tall hair came down close. "Is the agency working with our secret police?"

I hadn't a clue, couldn't believe anything Glasgow had said. I opened my mouth. The jaw ached as well. How many blows had he landed? All I had was a perverse sense of pride, Wall Street sort of pride, I might not be able to lick you, but I can lie your ears off.

I could tell him Maggie and Captain Hruby were warming each other's toes. Tell him his organization was leaking fore and aft, only a matter of time till the shock troops crashed in.

He was still close, staring into my face. He called, "Ludanyi!" and when the older man in shabby clothes came over, Cseve stood up. He walked around me, coat skirts flapping. "In a moment, I will turn you over to Ludanyi. He is a stupid peasant with no sense of the unique value of the individual." He hesitated. "I don't suppose you've read Locke? Ludanyi hasn't either. He is somewhat a sadist. I am certain he made your friends face him before he fired."

Like a bright dog, Ludanyi recognized his name. Each time he heard it, he nodded.

I wondered if I could get myself off the floor for one more try.

"You have ten seconds to tell the truth."

If Ludanyi marched me out, I might get a chance at him. He was older, not as fit-looking as Cseve. I might as well try.

József Cseve was still reading his watch.

I tried to speed him up.

"Go to hell," I said.

20

"*You will have* to forgive us. We are not medical professionals."

A hand dipped toward my face. I batted it away.

"Let him do it, for Christ's sake." Woman's voice.

The hand came back, pressed against the skin under my eye. "One more strip," Andras Kajdi said. I heard a snip. Fingers laid the tape across my nose, pressed the checks. The hands and the face above them were blurred. My nose and eyes were still running.

"If you can stand up, you can warm yourself," József Cseve said.

His men had rolled a barrel into the center of the room, lighted some scrap lumber. The ceiling was so high, and so many windows were missing, they didn't worry about the smoke. I wobbled within two feet of the barrel. It was throwing off enormous heat.

"We are not professionals," Cseve repeated, with a different emphasis, almost forlorn, as if he recognized a fatal flaw in that. "And you are not with the CIA."

"I'm an investment banker. Used to be."

"I lived in New York for two years," Cseve said. "They were putting your kind in jail."

Deborah Wolfe watched him walk over to his associates. She stepped near the fire and whispered, "We thought they'd shot you."

"You were in the truck?"

She nodded. "Andras was certain we were next. He told them we were just after a story."

Andras had taped my nose, so I couldn't think ill of him. But if the Holts or Smetana turned up, the shooting would be for real. In some fashion, they were professionals.

Ludanyi chuckled as he watched me approach. He said something to Cseve, who nodded and told me, "Professor Ludanyi says you will have eyes like a raccoon. He says we are making a ridiculous error in not shooting you."

"Do you plan to?"

"Kajdi I might be able to shoot." He looked across the room. "He is in bed with the secret police. Also, his propaganda plays are silly."

"You can't shoot all the informers in Hungary."

Professor Ludanyi said something. He understood some English.

"He says it would require dedication."

"You don't have time. This place is blown. You've got to know that." I felt absurdly grateful not to have been shot, warned myself not to identify too closely with my captors, Stockholm syndrome and all that. But it was in my own interest to get him to believe me. "Holt brought me down when he was lining it up," I said. "The CIA has been in and out. And the odds are good that state security knows. Kajdi was on the phone and got the location from someone. Your only bet is to get out of here."

Before Smetana and Holt come and shoot us. . . . Before you accept the necessity of doing it yourself.

He took too long thinking about it, and I prodded, "You can't do whatever you're trying to do from a jail cell." Though how this gang would do more than paint slogans on walls and overturn trash cans was beyond me. If you can't shoot a few people who get in the way, you're not serious about politics, or much else, I thought.

"You haven't asked what we are trying to do," he said.

"I don't care."

He stared at me with an evangelist's intensity, wanting to make his pitch to the unbeliever, to prove his case, whatever it might be, that Horthy was a sweetheart, that Himmler was unjustly maligned, I didn't know. Then he gave orders and things began to happen, not the things I wanted. Ludanyi opened double doors to a loading dock, went out and backed up the truck. There were forty or fifty crates and four men to load them, two to a crate. I crooked a finger at Kajdi.

"I will not!" he hissed.

"The sooner they're out of here, the better for us." The setup was so fishy I felt the skin on my neck crawling.

"I will not help arm fascists!" A little louder now. József Cseve looked around.

"Pretend it's boots for the poor. Pretend it's challah. Pretend it's any damn thing you want. If your friends in the secret police show up, there's going to be a shootout with us in the middle. You can phone in your report when Cseve's on the road."

"What do you think I am?"

A weasel. It wasn't the time to tell him. "An idealist who needs to live to write another play."

"I do *not* report to the secret police."

"I'm sorry. Help me lift the goddamn crates."

My right arm wasn't worth much, and Andras was little help. The conspirators loaded two boxes for every one Kajdi and I scraped aboard. After our second trip, he complained his back hurt and stopped to rest. I looked at my watch. He was waiting for something. There was no way he could have gotten in touch with anyone on the outside. Cseve's men had plucked the phone off him at the car.

Then it clicked. Kajdi hadn't expected to be at the factory.

He had expected to be nearby, where he could watch the action when the police stormed in. He would arrive to witness the arrests and have his exclusive for the *People's Voice*. That was why he wouldn't give up the press credentials; he had wanted to identify himself pretty soon.

"Come on," I said. I liked the idea of testifying that he had helped load the crates with nobody pointing a gun at him. Assuming I was in shape to testify.

We got another box aboard and I hauled him aside. "It must have worried you when no one responded to the shots."

"What do you mean?"

"Knock it off. When do they show?"

He pulled away.

I grabbed his arm. "If they come in shooting, you might look like one of the bad guys."

That offended him, that anyone could mistake Andras Kajdi— progressive journalist, socially responsible playwright—for a fascist. He had soaked it up at his mother's breast, or on his father's knee, whatever, thirty years after the fact—the dreadful goose-stepping past that must be reviled, the better world that could be found if you force-marched society down this other road.

"Just tell me this," I said. "Are we going to get out of here before the party starts?"

He jerked his arm free, went and stood by the barrel.

I returned to the truck and rescued my papers. Setting a crate on the floor, József saw me. "Your CIA credentials?"

I didn't know when. Soon.

I didn't know where. Inside the compound or outside the gate. Most likely inside.

He came over, flexing his hands. "Do you understand what is going on in Europe?"

"I don't care."

He knew I meant it, but he couldn't help himself. "It is reverting to tyranny. The old KGB-trained killers have come back, wearing a democratic face, some of them. There are new front men. Just behind them the old party apparatchiks remain. They are in the private sector as well. Your friend Kajdi's newspaper was purchased with party funds, and now it applauds the looting that goes on in the name of privatization, because the property is going to their friends."

"You sound like a man who's been cut out of the game."

"I do not enjoy watching murderers grow fat pretending to have discovered capitalism."

"They were elected, weren't they?"

"As reformers. Now they warn of resurgent fascism and use that as an excuse to shut down opposition newspapers, purge the radio and television. When this election comes, they do not plan to let go of power." He opened his fist and made a throwing-away gesture. It didn't matter what was being thrown away: something József Cseve and Professor Ludanyi and their friends didn't want to lose. The lot of them were like a political club that had talked too long about dangerous ideas.

"So you're going to hide a machine gun under your bed."

József Cseve shook his head. "We could not obtain machine guns. We have had to settle for rifles. Hunting rifles."

Too many thoughts came to sort out. First, that these bastards planned the kind of long-distance work that was so popular a couple of hundred miles south, against civilians. That Cseve imagined political targets, imagined himself and others setting up like Innes, taking shots at a dictatorial prime minister, or an interior minister, or heaven knew who else. I hoped the security forces crashed in soon. They belonged—

Except he had said *settled* for rifles.

"Have you had weapons training?" I said.

"We will have to learn."

"József, what did you do before you became a revolutionary?" He wouldn't like the word terrorist.

"I teach music. What does it matter? After tonight we will all go underground." He spoke with regret for whatever life he was leaving. So much more practical to have shot us. He read my mind and said, "Professor Ludanyi is more hardened that the rest of us. A few years before Kádár surrendered power, Ludanyi and several friends tried to start an opposition political party. Two friends were murdered, and Ludanyi was tortured. Would you like to know what they did?"

His eyes were feverish. I said, "Tell me."

"It is an old technique. A glass rod is inserted in the penis. The rod is then smashed." He clapped me on the shoulder, smiling at the corners. "Some of the people who did it still work for the Office for the Protection of the Constitution. If you're arrested, perhaps they will demonstrate for you."

"Maybe they'll demonstrate for Kajdi."

He shook his head. We both knew Kajdi wouldn't be arrested. "Who knows? If your human rights are abused, he may write a play expressing disapproval. But it will be a dilemma for him. There is a question, you see, whether fascists have human rights."

Cseve went back to work, and I joined the reporters at the barrel. As sorry as I felt for him, I hoped he never learned to be a good shot.

If I were in his place, I thought, I would take the next train to Vienna and get on with life. Leave the rodents to squabble over the cheese. They would always be there. But I'd had a hint why he couldn't do that, and I supposed if I had read John Locke I might have agreed.

It wasn't right to let the murderers grow fat. That was his point.

Andras was fidgety. It wouldn't be long.

There would be nowhere to hide in the building, and we would be exposed anywhere in the yard.

Not long, unless they planned to let this bunch go, follow them to other plotters. Or unless I'd completely misread things. As the last crates went aboard, Andras was jumping out of his shoes.

Lie flat and hope the ricochets missed.

And headlights flooded the yard, but that was because Ludanyi had started the truck and switched on the lights. The engine roared, sending clouds of exhaust back to mix with the wood smoke.

A horn beeped, too muted for the truck, and I walked over to where I could see the gate. There he was, the building's caretaker, Mihaly Mester, stumbling to open the gate for the black Mercedes that crouched with its high beams holding him as the horn bleated. The car swung into the yard. When the driver got out, he began arguing with one of József's men. The driver had long heavy arms, a mostly bald head, round face. Smetana. I took one look and went and snagged Wolfe's arm.

"Hey!"

"If you fuss, I'll leave you here." I moved us fast, toward the back wall. There was a ramshackle office back there, a dead end, but it was as far from the loading dock as I could get without kicking out a window frame.

"What are we doing?"

Also the stairs were here. Going up might not be a dead end.

"What about Andras?"

Kajdi was walking toward the dock.

"He's waiting for the cavalry. This isn't it."

No matter how soft in the head József Cseve might be, Erik Smetana was a professional and would insist on covering their tracks. I could have called to Andras, but that would have gotten Professor Ludanyi's attention. I wanted to fade, and be forgotten.

"Up."

There was a single light up there, on the second floor. It was quiet—the truck's rumble muffled—and feathers of bitter wood smoke rose across the stairway light. We could go up to the third floor. If they searched, it wouldn't make a difference, second or third. But they would be in a hurry, and they might not search. They might assume we had gone out a window.

Smetana would be the only one determined to find us.

Seeing Andras Kajdi, he might decide there wasn't a moment to spare in leaving. Assuming he knew who Kajdi was.

With the truck rumbling, I wasn't worried about the sound of our steps. I scouted the floor in the gloom, steering clear of areas no light reached. My memory was vague. The place had been dilapidated, water-stained, with slicks of ice here and there.

But I couldn't picture the layout, floor by floor, of interior walls and support pillars, scrap piles and hoist chutes.

"Who," Deborah Wolfe demanded, "was that man?"

"He was lurking around the hotel when you interviewed Holt. His name is Erik Smetana. I guess you'd say an importer. He arranged the transit of guns from Holt's plan in Belgium." Impressive, when I thought about all those borders. I found an empty window on the east, took a quick sighting at an oblique angle down at the loading dock. Andras appeared to be conducting an interview of Smetana and József Cseve. I put his life expectancy at about thirty seconds and began feeling bad that I hadn't dragged him along. It wouldn't have worked, but I should have tried.

"You knew all about the weapons," she said.

"Not all about. I thought they were headed for Serbia or Albania."

"Smetana is with TACEM?"

I thought he was a free-lancer, but what did I know? "Ask Andras. His sources are better."

There was a *pop* down below and Andras crumpled on the yard. Smetana was holding a pistol. József Cseve was holding his head between his palms, shaking it as if it might come off.

I said, "We'd better find cover."

"What happened?" Her face was pale, mouth loose, because she knew.

"Don't think about it."

But she couldn't help it, and the dim smoky light reflected the sheen on her skin. Her breath came rapidly, and she began swaying, losing sight of things, and there was nothing to do as her eyes rolled back but grab the jacket and keep her from going down too hard. Get the head low and people who faint usually aren't out for more than half a minute. But that can seem like ages. I got her knees up, opened her collar. Ice would have been great but I didn't want to risk pulling it off the window ledge. I squatted next to her, cursing her stupidity and Andras's and listened for footsteps. There wouldn't be many places to search downstairs, mainly the office and the wreck that had been a toilet, and if Smetana decided to search and didn't find us there—and didn't assume we had made it outside—he would take a peek up here.

I got up and looked through the south windows. They ran the length of the building, and half of them had been punched out. Five feet below was the sloping roof of a narrow addition that must hold the office. Judging by the ripples, the snow covered corrugated tin. Even if we dropped to the roof and didn't fall straight through, we would still make a hell of a racket.

Few options. When I lifted Deborah Wolfe's head, her eyes came open. Her disorientation lasted only a few seconds, then she turned her face away from me and said, "They shot him, didn't they?"

"Smetana did. Where's your notebook?"

She wanted to mourn Andras, but I persisted and she got out the notebook. Small thing with a stiff paper cover. I tore two corners off, gave it back.

"We've got to get out of here. There's a third floor. Can you stand?"

Adrenalin was kicking in. I got her around to the stairway, which was lighted from above, and aimed her up. Went back pulling a handkerchief out, unscrewed the single bulb on the makeshift line. I had to nibble the edge of the paper so it would fit the socket. Pushed it in partway, then screwed the bulb in tight. No contact, no light, no sign of tampering.

When I got to the third floor, I did the same thing.

The stairway to the roof was wood. I couldn't remember how the trap door fastened, but my fingers found a slide bolt and I got it open and we made it onto the snowy roof under a starless sky that took all its light from the ground. There was nowhere else to go. There was nothing built-up to hide behind, no water tank or air conditioning plant. No means of retreat, if you didn't include falling three stories. I crouched trying to avoid the wind that drove gritty ice under my collar. Facing south, where the hills rose, it was impossible to tell which part of the lumpy darkness lay on which side of the border.

I crept over to the east parapet, stole a glimpse below. We would hear the truck rev when it left, but I wasn't certain about Smetana's car.

Searching the building would take flashlights and time. They would have lights but not time—I hoped. We couldn't be that important to Erik Smetana. I'd told Cseve the site was blown. Cseve would have told Smetana. But the gun-runner still believed that *he* was operating in secret. Otherwise there was no point in shooting Andras. If he needed a point. He might just be in the habit.

I got us positioned so we would be behind the door if it opened. A weapon of any sort would have made me feel better. If he came up, I would try smashing the door down on him. A fall might break his neck. Christmas might come in March.

I heard the rotors an instant before light swept a corner of the roof, long enough to quash the urge to duck. We weren't in the light and the only thing that would give us away was motion. The gunship swept over, the searchlight targeting the yard. Deborah cringed.

I could tell from the noise that trucks were arriving. Shooting erupted. I wanted to see what was going on but stayed put. Fifty feet off the parapet, the helicopter hung at eye level while a soldier trained a stream of machine gun fire at the ground.

Andras's friends had come late.

Four corpses, if you counted the old superintendent just inside the gate. Kajdi in the yard where Smetana had shot him. Professor Ludanyi and a city man whose name I had never heard. Two prisoners, not in sight.

"We owe you and Andras an enormous debt," Captain Hruby said.

Soldiers and policemen swarmed over the property. From somewhere a briefcase of papers had appeared, including a manifesto that Hruby translated for us in stumbling English. "Absolutely shocking! Look at the swastikas! These people were loyal followers of Adolf Hitler!"

"Really." I guessed Cseve would have been born about ten years after the war ended.

"Oh, yes, really," he said.

Another van rolled into the yard. Two men in civilian clothes unloaded television cameras and lights. Hruby strode to meet them. He wanted the word out on the fascist insurgency. Deborah Wolfe raced to get in on the interview, passing within twenty feet of Kajdi's body before she jolted left, with an involuntary glance away, and took a less direct course.

I went inside. We had been coaxed down from the roof, and I had had plenty of time to look around. Now I wanted to make sure. I roamed through each floor. No police above the first level, though they had swept through. I hadn't heard any shooting from inside the building, but I might not have been able to tell. I went through the second floor and the third, unrigging light sockets, looking for another body.

Smetana was there, on the third floor, crouched in the shell of a collapsed chimney, pointing a Luger at my face.

21

"They'll hear the shot."

He knew it was true, but he didn't lower the gun. If they heard the shot they would come for him, to kill him or parade him. I thought he knew it was true. He hadn't fired. It was too dark in the hole to read his expression. The only thing the eyes showed was determination.

If he pulled the trigger, they would come. If I ran off, they would come. A dilemma for a man accustomed to the shadows.

"Go ahead then," I said. "They've killed most of the others."

"I can tell them things." He had made his decision. Better to be wrung out and paraded than shot.

"What can you tell them?"

He prodded the air with the gun. "I know names. You go tell."

"What names?"

"Conspirators!" He was nervous enough to shoot. Then he would have to go tell himself.

"Try one on me." He made a strangled noise, and I said quickly, "They'll want to know you've got the goods."

"A Hungarian who calls by the name Innes. Works for important man. Go tell."

I went down the stairs. None of the uniformed men or women I approached in the factory spoke English. I went outside and lured Captain Hruby away from the media. The camera aimed down at the bodies on the pier, which had been arranged side by side, hands folded, faces covered with jackets. I saw József Cseve, head bent, left arm bloody, being questioned beside a tank. I was glad he had survived.

"The guns' supplier," I told Hruby, "is hiding on the third floor. He says he can identify other conspirators." I told him where.

Hruby waved up a small squad and took off double time, fog pluming around their heads.

"Do you want a lift to your car?" I asked Wolfe. She had her back to a jacket-draped figure on the ground. Her knees were trembling.

I got her into Smetana's Mercedes and got us out the gate past secret policemen who were best friends with the news media. A salute, a wave, pass dear friend, and we'd covered less than half the distance to her car when she said, "I can drive."

"All right."

We stopped on the high road and traded the Mercedes for her Panda and she set us on the road north. I used half my attention on the mirrors. There wasn't much traffic, and we would stand out if Hruby changed his mind about letting an unreliable version of the story come out. Maybe Smetana knew Innes was out of the picture, maybe he didn't. Either way, Captain Hruby would want to check higher authority before tainting the name of the country's number one philanthropist. We reached the Hotel Corvinus in the early morning. I got out of the car and she stayed behind the wheel. She had kept her thoughts pretty much to herself, for which I was grateful. What could she say? Awful place, cruel people, dirty game.

She said, "Are you going to warn the Holts?"

"What?"

"The security forces will be after them."

"They can look after themselves." Besides, I didn't believe it, didn't believe one-tenth of it. I had read carefully the corporate profiles that Timmy Upham had sent, and the list of arms that TACEM produced didn't include sporting rifles. Machine guns, grenade launchers, mortars, tank killers—TACEM sold a few of them to special NATO units and moved the stuff by the ton in the Middle East. But not sportsmen's high-powered rifles. I didn't know where they had come from, wasn't by nature a gun buff. But I'd had a client in Westchester who couldn't stop boasting about the fancy new scope he had bought for his deer rifle, finest lenses made, couldn't produce that quality in the States, best ones came from Hungary.

She drove off, and I went up to the room and paced, back and forth because there wasn't enough room to follow my thinking around in circles. I had a couple of suspicions. It was too late to do anything about them. I lifted the phone and tapped the Burly Burgers number.

"Hello."

Male voice.

"Don't cut me off, you little shit."

"Actually, Miss Glasgow wants to talk to you." Recognized the voice a little, thought it was Carl's, wondered how he fit in; too old for her Scout troop. "Where will you be in thirty minutes?"

"At my hotel."

"I'll tell you where to meet us."

"Forget it. I'll be *here*." Harder for them to arrange fancy needle work. "Down consorting with the whores."

Left it to him to decide whether I thought he and Maggie would fit right in.

A convention of German pederasts had landed, and the girls were stuck three and four to a table while the Teutons sat among themselves. I got an empty seat at the farthest end from the bar, where all I could see one floor below was the avenue, nothing of the hotel's entrance. There was plenty to watch on the street. A drunk was trying to climb a snowbank and kept sliding back into the street. The taxi drivers were pretty decent about missing him.

A girl came over, blond with baby doll lashes and a mouth

full of discouragement, and made a perfunctory mime: free chair there, she'd noticed, but a dagger-shaped thumb jabbed at the Germans, maybe I was one of them. I shook my head. She took it as a possible yes and sat down with her legs already crossed. The waitress showed up right away. I should have realized. It was a whole town of pimps.

She wanted a champagne cocktail, my girl did, and as I had twenty thousand of Holt's dollars, if the check cleared, I let her. And one for me. We would toast the success of commerce among the formerly benighted, salute the deft fellows who had gone from Lenin to free markets in one step, keeping Captain Hruby around lest malcontents tried to spoil the game.

They showed up, all three of them, when we were on our second round and the girl was crossing and uncrossing her legs to show what a thousand forint would buy. "Chase your honey away," Carl said, "and start talking."

"She'll think we're with the Germans."

He gave her five hundred forint and made shooing gestures. Jeremy Butts brought up chairs for himself and Maggie. Carl sat on the girl's chair without checking it.

"If you stay here long enough," I said, "you start pimping your sister."

"My sister's got someone." He gave me a level stare. "You're especially full of shit tonight. We've been monitoring signals for fourteen hours. What the hell have you been up to?"

He hadn't said whose signals. I said, "Helping someone paint the tape."

"Talk sense."

Two hits of fizzy wine had left me lightheaded. My nose and my arm ached. The room was too vivid. Its reflective surfaces—the floor-to-ceiling windows, the chrome, the glasses—held too many images. But noting that Maggie and her boys looked ragged made me feel better. It was possible I knew more about what was going on than they did. József Cseve had told me what was in the crates.

"It's an old stock market term," I said. "It means creating an appearance of activity where there isn't much."

Glasgow looked at my glass with an expression that said she understood, I had been chugging champagne all day.

So I said, "The invoice from TACEM will say machine guns, won't it?"

"I doubt there will be an invoice," Carl said.

"Those gun-buyers were a conspiracy of idiots—or at least not your usual revolutionaries. A college professor, a music teacher and a couple of businessmen, as far as I could tell. A few losers who were worried about Communists returning, and took a shipment of rifles."

"Bullshit," Carl said.

"The Communists," Glasgow said patiently, "no longer exist."

"And state security watched every step of the way. When it was time to reel the villains in, Hruby even told reporters where to catch the action."

They traded glances.

"So a few months before the election, we've got a dramatic raid on an arms warehouse used by fascists plotting a coup. Captain Hruby's people or the Prime Minister's were onto the thing from the start. It may even *be* their thing."

Maggie shushed Carl. "Go on," she said.

"They had Milo Sipos reporting to them. They had Terrence Innes."

"Innes?" Carl laughed. "You're out of your mind."

"Here's a sophisticated guy, knows finance, able to pass for an Englishman, handy with a long-distance rifle—and he's cast his lot with József Cseve? Not a chance. He'd go for the winners."

I hadn't seen Magdalena Glasgow angry before. Disgusted, plenty often; stricken, just once, but not white-lipped and trembling. She said, "He killed an American agent to protect the conspiracy."

"I was there. He wanted the operation to keep running for a while. That isn't the same as protecting it." When none of them answered, I added, "You weren't coordinating with Hungarian intelligence. This was their operation, and Sampson got in the way."

They left a minute later. Rather, Glasgow stalked off wearing a look of pale murder, and Carl and Jeremy Butts chased after her. Letting the kid go first, Carl leaned across the table and said, "John Sampson was her favorite."

I didn't answer.

It hadn't been personal when Innes blew us off the road.

Nothing personal when Cseve's friends were gunned down. You only needed one or two plotters for a televised confession. If you put too many of these clowns in front of a camera, one of them might want to read from Locke and a few people in the audience might wonder why.

Hruby wouldn't know how much I had guessed. Getting me out of the picture wouldn't be his top priority. But sooner or later it would occur to him that I had ceased being useful.

"This isn't a great place to talk," I told Chester Holt.

He had been awake, not surprising, and had come downstairs to the Corvinus's lower lounge. The Gypsy violins had called it a night an hour or two ago. So had the drinkers, the bartender, and anyone who would have worried me hanging around in the lobby. Not a great place, but as long as Hruby's men weren't storming through the doors not a bad one.

"Has Smetana called?" I said. That was what he had been sitting up waiting for, an update from his arranger. The arranger, I thought, who had talked József Cseve into accepting hunting rifles for his freedom fighters instead of TACEM's machine guns, which Smetana would have shipped straight to the Balkan peninsula.

Chester tapped his fingers together. "It's a little late, young man, for riddles." But he didn't go back to his room to wait. He knew I knew something, that he was sitting up at three a.m. waiting for Smetana's call, and by implication that the call should have come earlier, and he wanted to know if I knew more without incriminating himself.

"If he does call," I said, "he will have switched sides and will be working for the National Security Office."

"I can't say I know them."

"Or perhaps it will be the Office for Constitutional Protection."

"Well, I'm sure they all do a fine job." If he had weighed fifty pounds less, he would have been out of the chair and moving. He gave an experimental rock forward.

"They're pretty efficient. When they arrived at your warehouse a couple of hours ago, they straightened things out right away. Shot a few people, took a couple of prisoners. Let the television crews get footage. I'm not sure how they handled Erik Smetana, but the last I saw he was offering to talk."

Holt teetered on the edge of the chair, muttering a string of homilies. The only words I caught were "treacherous bastard."

"Have you done business with him for long?"

"Wilkes has. Until now, Erik has been a reliable source of revenue for one of our companies."

"For TACEM."

He didn't seem surprised that I knew, but he bristled at what he heard in my tone. "There will always be wars, my friend, because man is inherently cruel. The people to whom we've sold weapons have reveled in bloodshed throughout recorded history. If TACEM and assorted Czech and Slovakian competitors didn't provide modern means, the combatants would bludgeon one another with rocks and tree limbs."

"Who got you in on the Hungarian deal?"

"Jim Wilkes, through Erik, of course."

"No, I mean who approached Smetana?"

"Mr. Innes."

It explained a lot. Smetana thought Innes was working with the Cseve group.

"Why all the rigmarole," I said, "in approaching Gabor's company, negotiating a factory?"

"Mr. Innes said it had to look arm's length, with a man notoriously difficult to approach. He had to protect himself, you understand. The arrangement was well thought out. Nobody could link Mr. Innes to the rifles."

"Where is the real stuff going?"

"South, my boy. Does it matter?"

"No." He wouldn't believe that he had been kidded twice, and to separate ends, by Smetana and Innes. Smetana had two sets of customers. Innes couldn't have cared less about wars to the south.

"We couldn't simply ship arms from Belgium," he murmured. "Good God, the Hungarians are nosy about what comes across their borders! But a plant to make small engines would receive deliveries of equipment, parts, lubricants—all routine. It becomes a small matter to offer an honorarium for an expedited review at customs if the paperwork is in order. The shipment south is less difficult. It is amazing what moves down the river under what guises." He saw me doing it. "You seem to be glancing at the door. Should we be expecting the authorities?"

"It seems likely."

"But it depends, doesn't it, on what Erik says?"

"Only how soon they come. Your deal was blown from day one. It was a setup. Innes was working for the government."

"Oh, my." He didn't have a Hoosier saying to cover the situation. But he wasn't stunned into paralysis. He was thinking, and it only took a moment. He bounded from the chair with a young man's energy. "Come with me." At a house phone, he punched a number that rang for a long time. "James, dear boy! Rouse your driver and get down to the plant as fast as you can. Charity and I will follow by taxi. A technical problem, but it needs attention." He depressed the lever, murmuring to himself, tapped another number. "It's me. Begin packing, but limit yourself to essentials, my dear. Patrick has brought some disturbing news, and he and I will be up in a minute." He hung up. "My wife may prove stubborn about abandoning a project. A few words from you should suffice."

"I gather you're not heading for Baja?"

"Young Jim may distract the authorities if they intercept him. And, of course, if Charity and I are free we can bring pressure to extricate him."

"Of course."

In the elevator, he said, "Why did you decide to warn us?" Straightforward for Chester, no "young man," no aphorisms, no coy simpers.

"If state security can't get to you, they'll have less on me."

"Ah, yes. Self-interest makes the world go round."

He had a suite that could have swallowed my room and still had space for testing small firearms. Two bedrooms, a sitting room with a view of the dazzling lights of the Chain Bridge, a fax machine on a table near the window, an exercise cycle in a corner. Charity Holt burst out of one of the bedrooms, face dark, hair like a lacquered black helmet. She was dressed in clothes that didn't become her: turtleneck, sweat pants, lug-soled shoes—everything in black, the kind of getup you would don if you expected to make the next border crossing on foot after midnight. She threw a small soft-sided bag on the floor, put her fists on massive hips. They don't paint fireplugs black, or add rouged faces, but the resemblance was strong. The checkered butt of a handgun peeked from the bottom of her shirt.

"How much does this bastard know?" she snapped.

"Our problem, dearest, is what the secret police know. They may have Erik in custody."

She gave me a scrunched look of hatred that had a lot of calories behind it. "Who betrayed him?"

Long story. He cut it short. "Jim Wilkes will be driving down to Baja. As soon as he leaves the hotel, we will hire a cab. The

Slovakia border is eighty kilometers. Unfortunately, it is marked by a river, so we will have to attempt a legal departure."

They wouldn't stand a chance. Crossing points would be on alert.

Charity Holt was doing some thinking. She said, "Your weakness, Chester, is that you're too willing to see only the best in your fellow human beings. This louse, for example"—no question who—"has been double-crossing us from the get-go. I'm not sure just *how*, but I know a double-dealer when I see one."

Chester looked at me with wounded eyes. "I *do* like to assume people are square."

I had had enough. "Square like sending Wilkes down to Baja?"

"Now that's a case of necessity. Sometimes necessity takes the front seat."

Charity said, "I wouldn't bet this bastard isn't the one who ratted us out."

I leaned against the sofa. Couldn't remember last sleeping, but it had been less than twenty-four hours. I said, "That's nice church social talk, 'ratted us out'."

Chester gave me a wink. "Now, bub, let's not get started."

"He'll sell us out as soon as we're on the road."

I didn't bother asking why she thought I had warned them. Then Chester said, "We'll ask him to accompany us," and I knew I should have raised the objection.

"I can't accompany you," I said. "Besides—"

He smiled at his wife. "And why not?"

"For one thing, I've still got business here. For another—"

"Pooh! You can't tell me your little effort can't be abandoned. What's the other reason?"

"I don't think you've got much chance of getting across the border. I wouldn't bet you'll get a mile outside Budapest. Either way, if Charity decides to shoot it out, being around you won't be healthy."

"A sniveling regard for your skin, then?"

"That's right."

"Beware the man who appears candid," Chester said. "I have to compliment my wife on her instincts about people. Is it possible that our young friend envisions a role for us similar to the one I've devised for Wilkes?"

Charity's head snapped up and down. "You've put your finger on it, Chester."

His lower lip pushed the upper one almost into his nose. For a guy who assumed people were square, he came to the opposite conclusion about me with little struggle. He took a brocaded pillow off the sofa. "My dear? One can't carry a traitor in the family car. And we can't leave him behind." It was only after he had handed her the pillow and she pulled the gun that I caught the drift.

22

The train compartment door slammed, and Peter Rice came partly awake and said, "Fucking racket."

"It was next door."

He raised the sleeping mask, squinted and found nothing to his liking. The compartment was full of morning light. That wasn't an improvement. The shabbiness of the seats and floor hadn't jumped out at me when we caught the first train out at the Eastern Station in Budapest at six a.m.

The train was snaking on an electrified track through a mountain valley, and for miles ahead the land continued to rise. There had been towns along the way, and a fair-sized city. I had been watching since the sun came up. The compartment's heat had come on a bit at dawn. My feet no longer were numb, and I could move without creaking.

"Your clients didn't tell me the truth last night," he said.

"They told you some of it."

"This Smetana—he's fixed up other sales for Holt, is that right?"

"Yes."

He pulled the mask off, rubbed his palms against his forehead. "They've done it all before, yes? But Mum and Da—and charming people they are—have never set up a phony industrial company as a front, have they?"

"They said this deal would be worth their while. Several million dollars."

He stretched and groaned, patted down his beard, sucked his teeth. Not someone you would want to wake up with regularly. He was putting on the show partly to pay me back for rousing him from his bed at five a.m. with the promise of a hell of an exclusive story.

"I've been thinking, as I often do while asleep. Why didn't the security police take the Holts into custody at the time of the Baja raid? If you're right about Innes, your Captain Hruby knew what they were doing from the start, from the get-go, as the lovely hag likes to say."

He hadn't known Charity long enough then to call her a hag. But he was right. Smetana could swallow his tongue or hang himself with his shoelaces, and Hruby still had enough to arrests the Holts.

"Hruby doesn't want too many witnesses," Peter said. "That could be good for us or bad. If I were Hruby, I think I would expect the Holts to keep their mouths shut if they made it out of the country. But would I count on it?"

"Let's hope."

"Would I count on *you*, and Deborah Wolfe, to keep quiet? If I know Andras's playmates, I imagine they have exactly what they want. A whole Nazi cabal, with ties to Americans who most certainly work for the CIA. Armed with a few confessions, the Prime Minister, a lovely man and a humanist, will be able to whip up nationalist hysteria before the election. It's a pity Andras isn't around to appreciate the show."

When I didn't comment, he said, "I could decide that *you* are more dangerous to be around than the Holts."

"No so." I'd told him how close it had been in the hotel room, how slowly they'd agreed there might be a better way out than shooting me. We had spent the hours between three-thirty and five-thirty at Dolce Vita, Milo's favorite stripper bar. When Milo and I were there, it had been nearly empty. The small hours had brought out half the town's visiting businessmen, and the girls were doing better than the skyway workers at the Corvinus.

Chester's biggest challenge at the szex club was taking in the sights without seeming overly interested. It was easy to read his disappointment when Charity shooed away would-be lap dancers. He had said pensively, "They achieve a level of detachment that is unknown in most human activity," which told me he had not only been watching but also imagining.

I was the one who came up with the idea of hiring two girls to accompany us on a brief tourist excursion. The transaction was fine with management, which advertised Dolce Vita as an escort service as well as "erotisches lokal" show. Four hundred dollars per day per escort, payable to the manager. Chester pushed up the lower lip and counted out sixteen fifty-dollar bills.

Neither girl spoke much English. Neither had an aversion to "Papa" Chester. Once Charity saw the logic of the arrangement, she promoted me from traitor to ally. Józsefne had dyed red hair—red like Christmas tinsel—and a drugged vacuity that promised no trouble as long as she kept herself happy. Ida was a miniature with black bangs and the predatory speed of a forest feeder. First chance, I planned to empty her purse and pockets of nail files. Bundled in their thin coats in the taxi with us, they completely changed our group's profile. We were no longer three fleeing criminals but a happy extended family.

At Keleti Palyaudvar, the Eastern Station, Peter had the compartments booked when we arrived. Charity took the girls into the ladies room and brought them back with their faces scrubbed, looking clean if unhealthy. As long as they kept their coats buttoned over the gaudy dresses, they could pass for family. If the sleeping arrangements surprised Ida, she didn't let on. I was welcome, she made it plain, to join her and Józsefne in a threesome, or to watch them if that was my preference. I smiled at the wild animal back in her eyes and motioned regrets and hoped the compartment Peter and I shared had a good lock. Putting Ida among horny businessmen was like putting a snake down a mousehole. I felt guilty about the risk I had imposed on unsuspecting conductors. As their door closed, the small dark creature was moving on Józsefne. Peter and I sat with the Holts for forty minutes as he got an antiseptic version of their adventures and I listened for screams next door. The sun hadn't come up when we decided to try for a couple hours' sleep.

I had gotten at least twenty minutes' worth before the sun began blinding me.

Peter adjusted his rumpled suit, did up buttons, snugged his tie. "We should be in Miskolc in fifty minutes. Then we have two choices. There is a border checkpoint about sixty kilometers northwest. We can go by car—there *may* be transportation standing by in Miskolc. Tell me, Patrick?"

"Yes."

"Have the Holts sworn off shooting their problems?"

"I wouldn't count on it."

"Is the fat lady still armed?"

"Both of them are."

"I'd hate to have us all get across into Slovakia, then have them decide to suppress their story."

Once they had eluded state security, a self-serving change of heart was a risk.

Peter said, "We could send them across on their own, on foot. The frontier normally is pretty porous up there. There's a river, the Sajo, but it comes miles before the crossing. The other choice is the airport at Miskolc. I've gone out of there once."

"What's Miskolc like?"

"Industrial, pretty as Birmingham on a rainy day." He heaved himself up, rolled out into the corridor. The toilet was at the downwind end of the car. He came back in five minutes. "The tarts are out soliciting passersby. We may get arrested for procuring instead of gun-running."

"Is it even illegal?"

"Let's see if they're serving breakfast."

The dining car was empty, the tables stripped. En route we

ran into Ida, who was wearing the same pink evening dress as the night before. She made "what gives" gestures and said, "Chester Papa?"

Peter said something in Magyar and explained to me, "I told her Chester's got the flux but hopes to avail of her services soon."

She shrugged and went on prowling the carriage.

"There's another problem," Peter said, sitting at a bare table. "Your embassy won't want to embarrass the current government."

I hadn't told him about Glasgow, or what had happened to Innes and Sampson, no reason to, the story hung together without complications. I said, "I don't think the embassy will mind seeing the government in trouble."

"You don't know the score. London and Washington both love the current Prime Minister. He's a technocrat, type fellow who helped make the Berlin Wall obsolete. The only fear the West has is that he will play the irredentist card too hard, raise too much of fuss about the Romanians' treatment of their Hungarians, maybe, or if the economy keeps sinking, get some shooting started to distract the masses. The fact that he and his private Stasi have this place nicely zipped up is an internal affair."

He saw my expression and said, "Look, my friend, the Russians *buried* Chechnya, made the fifty-six uprising here look like a cricket match. What changed? Nothing. Yeltsin still represented stability in Russia. It'll be the same here. Diplomats go for stability every time, saves them learning a new pecking order. While you were out playing last evening, where do you think I was?"

"I don't know."

"Your ambassador invited the press in for a private, informal dinner at home. Message was, couldn't we do something to buff up the image of this government? It's no pack of ideologues, look at the reforms and so forth, good people."

The ambassador wouldn't have known, I thought, wouldn't have known about Maggie Glasgow's operation or its casualties.

"The point," Peter said, "is that I want to get the Holts on tape, then get myself and the tape out of here. There are three or four newspapers that would love the story, and a couple of radio programs, but I can't file it from Budapest."

I went with him down the corridor, and he rapped at the Holts' compartment.

Chester and Charity were dressed but disheveled and querulous. Peter sat down across from them, switched on his recorder. "Here's where we get down to cases. In return for my assistance, I expect—"

"Turn that goddamned thing off," Charity snapped.

Peter left the recorder running. "I believe we'll have transportation waiting at the next station. From there the big question is whether we can pass ourselves off as innocents. If the word's out on you, there's nothing we can do if someone demands papers. On the other hand, the security people may be keeping this to themselves. I propose we head for the airport."

"You said there are commercial flights?"

"Lots fewer than from Ferihegy, and not on airbuses. But we could get something to Vienna. And it wouldn't be alarming if a group of rich Americans chartered a plane."

From what I could see through the window, we had gotten into the industrial area, with electrical towers and squat factories breaking the blue-white wasteland of snow. Holt's face glistened in the light. He said, "Is there another way across?"

"If you can hike five miles, yes. Let's go over what we talked about last night."

"So that's the price of our ticket? You drive a hard bargain." Holt's forced cheerfulness told me that given a choice, he would return to escape plan A, without witnesses.

There were police at Miskolc station, two blue uniforms on the platform, two leather coats twenty feet from the main doors.

"If they were sure," Peter said, drawing back from the

window, "they would have men storming aboard. There'll be more in the station, probably a carload of them out front." He eyed our two escorts and shrugged. Charity had had more time to work on the girls, and their hair was combed out and tied in demure ribbons, mascara and nail polish gone. They were as convincing as possible in spike heels. The police would notice the heels.

Peter sighed. "Nothing for it," he said. He stuffed his computer bag under the seat across from Chester.

He got off first, alone. The row started a few seconds later.

Once onto the platform, Ida and I hooked arms. Józsefne, the younger daughter, was getting off with Mama and Papa at the other end of the carriage. I wondered if she remembered Peter's instruction to chat merrily to her folks about university life. More of Chester's money had changed hands. The girl's reluctance melted. She was all animation. God knew what she was saying about higher education, and in what accent.

We had to step aside as Peter and one of the uniformed men shouldered their way to the train. The leather coats were paying less attention to us than to Peter. He switched from Hungarian to high-pitched English sarcasm. "Fucking bloody thieves—need it for my work—can't get a laptop like that in this pestilential hole," and so on.

We entered the station. The floor was gritty, the window panes were cracked beneath old filth.

Ten steps.

The man who was waiting looked away.

I didn't let on that I had picked him up, but the whole picture had changed.

The bastard had been following ahead, had given himself away only by pivoting a few degrees for a quick check that we were still with him. Drooping mustache, bony nose, lantern jaw, big cheeks, coal black eyes. Clumsy of him to let me see him after he had driven the Holts and me to Baja for the Europa Foundation. The fellow Holt kept calling called Steve.

István.

We got out the front door, the two Holts, their daughters and me, and I waved up a taxi. It wasn't the transport Peter had promised, but it would have to do.

I gave the taxi driver the address Peter had written down. Hotel Pannonia, Kossuth utca. The center of the city looked thinly populated. Office workers were at their desks, and it was too cold for shoppers. There was a fair amount of automobile traffic on the main streets, and I couldn't tell whether anyone was following. We lost some other cars at a light, and that let me concentrate on the four vehicles that remained with us. Windshield reflection hid one of the drivers. Two others were women, not conclusive, and the fourth was an old man. One of the women drivers had two male passengers who were looking everywhere except at us. One of the passengers was István.

I settled back. It was tight in the rear seat with Charity at the one door and the girls stacked between us. Every time we swerved, Ida balanced herself with a tiny hand on my thigh, trying to get something going. I don't know what she expected.

The light changed, and the blue Escort with the indifferent passengers scooted off ahead of us but never got far ahead. The fact István hadn't whistled up the security police at the station should have told me something. All I let myself think was that for some reason they didn't want to roll us up yet—or didn't have the manpower in the neighborhood.

If they had only one surveillance vehicle, we had a fair chance of losing it. Peter's instructions had made sense, though they left me wondering how often a reporter had to ditch surveillance. If we were well covered, he said, there wouldn't be much we could do.

So we swung into the driveway in front of the Hotel Pannonia, the driver pointing ahead helpfully, saying something that meant here we were or tips were welcome, and the car bearing István, which was fifty yards ahead, was supposed to keep going on the one-way avenue, circle the block, come round, find us and our taxi gone.

The first sign it wasn't working was a squeal of tires down the street. The Escort had spun halfway around in the skid, and the tires were spinning as the engine raced until the rubber found traction and they shot toward us against traffic that bleated and dodged.

I was out of the taxi by then. Chester Holt had one foot out. The girls were scissoring their way across the seat. Ida climbed out first, impervious to her surroundings, and tried to cling to me.

The woman driving the Escort was steering out of a skid at the hotel entrance, bumping the left rear wheel over the curb as the other tires got a piece of the driveway. She wore a navy beret, bouncing hoop earrings, and dark gloves that appeared now and then at the top of the steering wheel. The Escort was still moving, the engine still whining, when István spilled out on the passenger's side and I understood they weren't following Peter's script at all, no discreet arrests, this was going to be noisy. István lifted a machine pistol and looked for targets as a larger, round-faced man jumped out on the opposite side with an automatic shotgun.

The shotgunner was still clearing his door when his face speckled red and Chester's gun went *pok-pok*.

I pushed the girl away from me.

She twisted, tangling our feet.

István opened up on the taxi. Windows blew, red mist sprayed everything.

I tried to get my head down.

Chester killed the woman behind the wheel.

I scuttled for cover on hands and knees.

Charity was out, filling the opposite doorway, small pistol snapping. István fired another burst. The old woman dropped back into her seat.

I was working toward the rear of the vehicle. Under my

hands was an angular thing with Christmas tinsel hair and an empty face. I didn't know how she had got there. I crawled on. When I reached the rear bumper I looked back. Chester was crouched behind a door, getting protection from the coachwork and the engine, firing spaced shots across the right fender.

He called out, "My dear?" without looking around.

István fired a string that took out the last of the windows. On my belly, I saw a doorman hiding at the hotel entrance. Another man was dashing along the building.

"My dear?" Chester's voice was plaintive. "Are you all right?"

Ida scrambled past me, black bangs swinging, a garish grin below the mad eyes. Ten feet behind the taxi was a column supporting the porte-cochère. It looked solid. In any case, it was a place to go and she went.

I couldn't see István or much else. Chester crouched and waited. Under a door I saw the shotgunner. To my right was Józsefne. The taxi's exhaust pipe sputtered.

Only seconds had passed. There were no sirens hee-hawing in the distance. No screams. None of the traffic on Kossuth had stopped. Only seconds, and there were minutes to go before any intervention arrived, and then it wouldn't be on my side. The standoff between István and Chester Holt would be over before then.

I looked under the cars and still couldn't spot István.

"My dear . . . ?"

Holt's whine. I hadn't taken more than two breaths since his last cry.

I crossed behind the taxi, risked a glance along the left side. The rear door was open, and a plump shoeless leg hung out.

A flicker of movement, not from the leg but forward and higher, the driver's head. I could see only a crescent of black hair low against the seat back. The head moved again, turning a few degrees.

If you're awake, put the car in gear and hit it. Get yourself out of here.

Something hissed. Ida was behind the column. Anywhere she moved from there would expose her. But she had gotten the best cover she could. She saw me looking and jabbed a finger at the ground beside her.

I nodded but stayed put. I could retreat straight down the driveway for a reasonable distance using the taxicab and István's acute angle to protect me. Didn't need to draw fire so Ida could scoot away.

He shot through the empty windshield frame and the driver's movements stopped.

No question who was going to win the standoff. Chester had gotten lucky because two of the opposite team hadn't been prepared for an old man's patient marksmanship.

"Charity, dear?"

It occurred to me that I could help myself by helping him. I edged past the rear fender. The cars faced one another at a slight angle, like clock hands pointing to five after six. Most of the doors stood open. As a result, I had to get father than I wanted from the body of the taxi in order to get István's attention. When I looked past the edge of Charity's door the first time, I caught a glimpse of István before he noticed me. He had both feet on the Escort's chassis and was supporting himself from the door post, his six feet two or three scrunched up to present a small target while he aimed the machine pistol through two blown-out windshield spaces at Holt's position. The two men were no more than twelve feet apart. István had slightly better cover behind his dead driver.

He swung the pistol faster than I had expected, but I was behind the taxi before he could fire.

He would have to assume I was armed and was trying for a shot. All I had to do, in theory, was lean past the door and I had a half decent line of fire. He couldn't see my attack coming until the last instant. There wasn't much he could do about the situation, either. He could shoot through the sheet metal door now and then, hoping to hit an invisible target. He could try something fancy like shooting into the pavement in front of the door and hoping for a cute bounce. What he couldn't do was raise himself for a more useful shot over the door, or through its blown window, couldn't do that without exposing himself to Chester.

It seemed a long time as I waited behind the fender, but probably less than ten seconds passed before he spread four shots across the middle of the door. It was a waste of time, and I let him know it a moment later by a flash appearance. This time slugs tore up the entire rear quarter, took out the tire, blew concrete chips loose an inch from my foot, showered me with glass that I had thought was already gone.

I wanted to just hunch there. But it wouldn't do. I had set the thing up. Chester had to have gotten the idea, and I had to go through with it.

The next time I moved, István was ready. Whether he had spotted a reflection on chrome, or picked up a refracted shimmer in a bit of glass, or noticed a mottling on the pavement in the otherwise shadowless morning, he knew it was coming. If I hadn't pulled back at the last moment, he'd have torn me apart as he raised himself on the Escort and fired down through the window as well as poking holes in the door. Not quite lost in the chatter of his weapon was the closely spaced *pok-pok* nearby.

I braved a look under the door. István was down, wiggling to the back of the Escort, both legs moving but the gun arm holding his middle.

"Got him."

Chester's high-pitched report.

"He's moving."

Chester ignored me. He kept low as he waddled backwards. When he got to the rear passenger door, I was bent low on the opposite side. We both got a good look at Charity Dear at about the same time. Chester raised his gaze and met mine. He still had his blued little automatic. There was a look on his face. He had suspected me before of selling them out, and here we were again—in trouble—and here I was, and he just didn't have a homily that covered such treachery. Then as he brought the gun up, I saw I had misread him. At some level he believed his homemade quilt and canned-tomato bromides, believed Charity was Dear Charity, light of a lifetime, devoted confidante, only love without whom, whatever—and he put the gun in his mouth and in defiance of all the experts who said it couldn't be done shot himself twice.

I looked away, backed away, and walked into István's line of fire. He snapped off two but couldn't have been steady. Then I was out of sight behind the taxi, heading for the sidewalk. Ida was gone, not even a flapping coat to be seen. Still no police sirens. The white SE that hurtled down the street wasn't a police car. One of the hit squad had called for help. I paid the car no attention. Heard its tires squeal at the driveway. There were people running to the scene behind me. I didn't look. The bigger the crowd, the harder time the SE would have packing up István and his gun.

I turned off Kossuth. Two pedestrians ahead, an old woman and a young one going arm in arm, faces ducked against the cold, no one else even close, a man across the street limping into a restaurant, a truck double-parked at the end of the street with two men unloading. No police cars.

Finally, back on Kossuth utca, sirens, two or three whooping in different sequences.

I slowed, breathing hard, wondered what kind of appearance I made, noticed glass pebbles on my coat's left shoulder. Shook them off. I crossed the street. Passing the restaurant, I removed a glove, ran a bare hand across my face. It came away clean. I wasn't walking the town wearing a grinning bloody mask. Nose was taped. Hair okay, nothing the breeze couldn't have done, topcoat intact, trousers in one piece. A fair amount of Charity's blood had to be on my shoes, but I wasn't leaving tracks. I passed the men at the truck, who were busy arguing.

I kept walking.

□ □ □

An arm came out of the doorway, and I almost hit its owner. Peter Rice was standing next to her, next to Deborah Wolfe, his transport, of course. She must have set out driving this morning as soon as he had phoned.

"Where have you been?" she demanded.

"Have you got a car?"

"Where are the Holts?" Peter said.

I told him as we walked. Varoshaz ter, a bricked pedestrian square, seemed an inapt choice of rendezvous. It had been such a bad choice, I thought giddily, that only one of us had made it. The old buildings housed the town and regional government offices, and it was thick with police and other officious looking citizens. The square opened onto another pedestrian street, and a block later we slid into Wolfe's Panda.

"You look terrible," she said.

Wide-eyed and deranged possibly, as if I'd been crawling among corpses.

Peter was businesslike. "The man picked you up at the station?"

"Yes."

"So there was a car waiting for him and they followed you to the hotel—"

"Yes."

"And they waited till then to do the assassination, but still right out in the open. That's not the security police. Intensive interrogation would precede whatever else they did."

"They aren't interested in learning things. They *know*."

"Still not their style, the whole thing."

I thought he was overestimating their commitment to style. The siege in Baja hadn't relied on finesse.

"Besides which," Peter said, "you saw the official team at the station. The leather coats, just like the old days. If they'd made you, you'd have been arrested."

"Suppose they were there for spotting."

Wolfe had the engine buzzing but hadn't left the curb.

"I suggest we drive for the border," Peter said.

"You mean the airport."

"That was for the Holts' consumption. Our chances at the frontier are much better. We're three traveling journalists. Miss Wolfe and I are beyond reproach. No one has an interest in us. You'll be a problem."

"You may be a problem yourself."

"How's that?"

"There'll have been questions about the man who made all the fuss at the train station. The train conductor will remember that you spent time with the old American couple. Also, if they're doing their job back in Budapest, they'll have noticed that my friend Mr. Rice seems to have gone missing. Then it's a matter of someone noticing that Mr. Rice fits the description of the pisspot at the rail station, who helped the Holts slip through. From then on, someone will have an interest in you. In Debs, here, too, once they can't find her. She interviewed Holt, Cseve and for all the government knows, Smetana. In any case, she knows the raid was a setup."

She gave me an empty stare. "'Debs'?" She took a breath. "Talking to people is my job." She thought that what we were talking about was like a beef with the boss over an expense account lunch.

"They're out to control the spin, and you're as much an obstacle to that as I am."

She looked at Peter, who said, "Let's see first if we can get out of this town." He pulled a map from between their seats. He told me over his shoulder: "Two main roads lead northeast and northwest to crossings into Slovakia. No 3 east, No. 26 west. They're the most likely to be watched. Directly west, however, is an unpromising road through the Bukk Mountains. In the summer, the area is popular. In the winter, there are a few ski lodges. The roads should be lightly traveled. We should know if we have company. We can find an inn for a couple of days. The opposition will tell itself we made it to Vienna. That's when we go across, on foot if need be."

He brought up the Europa Foundation five minutes later. We were making good time, with no sign of a tail. "You say István drives for Europa? Makes one wonder who the others shooters work for." He decided to answer his own question. "Free-lance?"

Wolfe didn't take her eyes off the road. We were in a traffic circle that was mostly ice.

"I think," I said, "that Gabor's assistant was working with the secret police."

"Was?"

I told him.

He noticed the woman's silence. "Did you know this?"

"Patrick told me, Andras and me, last night."

"And you didn't tell your friend Peter?"

"I hadn't seen you since then. Innes would be worth a lot inside the foundation," she said. "The authorities would know what Mr. Gabor is up to, could influence his decisions."

Peter didn't answer right away.

She said, "Was Innes blackmailed, or bribed, or a believer?"

She steered us onto a two-lane road that ran straight through a wasteland of industrial plants and slag heaps. There was traffic, but I had been watching ahead and behind and hadn't spotted a white Mercedes. There was a truck directly behind us, following closer than I liked, pulling an open trailer loaded with some kind of smoldering rubbish.

Staring at the landscape, Peter said, "Dear me. It's difficult to blackmail a person these days, as so very little is forbidden. And hard to bribe somebody making the kind of money Gabor must pay.'"

Wolfe nodded. "Okay, then. If you were running things back when Communism was supposed to live forever, wouldn't you want to plant an agent on someone like Gabor?"

"I might."

"Who was in charge back then?"

"In Hungary? János Kádár," Peter said abstractedly. "Ran things for thirty-some years, played every side of the street, reliable Marxist, ran show trials, got a taste of it himself, turned the counterrevolutionaries over to the Soviets after fifty-six. Clever man. Liberalized the economy a bit later. It would be interesting to know when Innes joined Gabor's service. He *could* have been groomed by the intelligence services." He tilted back his seat. "I'd never put such guesswork in writing under my own name."

"All right, it's conjecture," Wolfe said. "Try some more. Innes is dead. He had people working for him. Who gives them orders now?"

"Captain Hruby," I suggested.

Peter was silent for a moment. "Why not Gabor?"

She glanced at him, and the car wiggled.

"One's as likely as the other, isn't it," Peter said. "Suppose young Tamás came to Kádár's attention. Or that of his intelligence chief. The boy's a genius. Good background, family left during the war. Tamás didn't get himself into trouble during the fifty-six uprising. What exactly did he do during that uprising, I wonder?"

"Inform?" Wolfe said.

"Perhaps . . . or worse. Young man in his early twenties might have put a hand in on one side or the other."

"So they spot his talent," Wolfe said. "Then what?"

"They educate him abroad. Provide seed money for his career."

We had lost the truck a mile back. The nearest car was a quarter mile behind us, and the road ahead was clear except for a rapidly dwindling minivan that had passed us a couple of minutes ago. I watched the van and thought about the way Innes had rushed to get ahead.

Peter resumed the discussion. "It's a question of whether we believe in Gabor's intelligence, isn't it? On one hand, we can believe that Terrence Innes was running a game right under Gabor's nose without the financial genius catching on. Or we can believe that Gabor is a lifelong opportunist who knows who his friends are."

The road had narrowed and begun to climb. We were outside the industrial belt, rising into heavily forested hills with stubby mountains ahead. Few factories now. Dirty snow hid the scars. The road forked, and Peter said we should go south. I felt easier. The trees closed in, and the road surface vanished under bumpy snow. Ice fenders lined the shoulders.

We came to a lodge in a mountain pass twenty minutes later, and they were waiting there under the snow-heavy conifers.

23

The minivan blocked the road and a battered Trabi squatted behind an outcrop of hillside. We couldn't see them until we came around a bend and started downhill, and by then the old Trabi was rolling across the road to cut us off. The road hadn't been plowed after the last couple of snowfalls. Its frozen ruts provided no traction.

Wolfe cranked the wheel left, and we clipped a fender of the Trabi. The Panda bounced sideways before the tires caught. Then we leapt off the road and into the drive at the front of the lodge. Nothing had been plowed here, nothing all winter, and the crisp snow scraped our fenders and undercarriage. She kept us moving, down along the right side of the closed building, losing momentum with every yard as the wheels spun harder and the tail sashayed, and then we were going nowhere. She shifted down and the engine screamed, and then she shifted higher and the tires caught a little something and we hit another slope down. She steered away from a drift that would have stopped us dead, bounced the left fender off a log post supporting a side porch, and then we were into the lee of the building.

It was a dead end.

Behind the lodge, and on the side, the land sheared away and the tops of pines seemed to float nearby. Wolfe spun the wheel again and stopped. We were nosed up against a stone outbuilding.

"Nice driving," I said.

"Oh!" A moan. Wolfe closed her eyes and opened them again. I had seen two men beside the minivan, couldn't tell how many were in the East German heap. It might take a minute for the men on foot to reach us. I rolled down the window and heard the whine of an engine. The Trabant was coming and would get here first.

I told her what was about to happen.

Peter said, "We could try to get into the building."

I was watching the corner of the lodge. There would be a flash of dull metal. No, first a flicker of shadow on the snow. The sun would throw their shadow ahead.

I said, "Now!"

The engine pitch rose like a drill, and the tires bit and we lurched backward as the Trabi driver's face grew in the near window. He didn't comprehend, even when we made the low-speed contact, rear bumper to side door, and she kept her foot down, adding a few miles an hour to his speed and changing his direction. There was no stopping either of us. The old Trabant reached the edge and kept going, and so did the Panda.

We went off about ten feet apart, which made all the difference. The Trabi slid into rocks about twenty feet downhill and stopped there. The Panda rolled onto its side and began spinning. A window burst and hard-packed snow poured in. Then a long slide, a half minute's worth at least, sledding upside down. A second of freefall. Impact forward and a half-flip. The rear came around and landed hard.

I couldn't tell if we were still moving.

Hazy blindness took over, because everything was white. Then a dark bonnet of hair sorted itself out, red knuckles. Empty window with trees. I twisted around until the seat was under me, and that made the trees right side up.

As soon as I crawled out the window I slid a dozen feet on glazed snow. The Panda's front bumper was decorated with a tangle of fir branches caked with ice. Beyond the car, far above it, the top of the hill was obscured by pine and deciduous trees. Off to the right was a rock promontory where the Trabi had hung up. We had come further than I would have guessed, several hundred yards, most of it on an incline that was almost vertical. Somewhere up there the Panda had gone airborne for a distance before slapping down like a ski-jumper. If we hadn't snagged rocks and flipped upright, the hood and roof would have carried us to the floor of the valley a quarter mile below.

I scrambled up to the car. Peter looked out dreamily. The left side of his face was bloody, the right side pristine except for wrinkles and beard. "I think I'd rather be shot here where I'm comfortable," he said.

"You'll get your wish."

Wolfe was holding a scarf under her nose. She undid the seat belt and worked the door handle. The handle turned but the door didn't budge. I reached in on Peter's side, fumbled with the lock. He stumbled out, sat down inadvertently and rolled until his weight broke the snow crust.

The sheet metal beside my head banged, and I went down hearing the shot. Wolfe fell out, crabbed toward the front.

The shooter was hanging onto a sapling, aiming his pistol again, and the thing fired but there was no sign of an impact. At this range, the first shot had been lucky.

The next person might have a rifle. Branches shook, someone stumbling handhold to handhold. The first man fired again, lost his balance and tumbled twenty feet. When he got to his knees, his hands were empty.

If we stayed put, they would come down to us or tear the slope apart with rifle fire. Some trace of survival instinct made me rescue the map from the car. Deborah Wolfe led the way downhill, running and sliding. Someone at the top with a machine pistol fired several long bursts before giving up. When I looked up from the bottom of the slope, neither shooter was in sight. When Peter caught up, I handed him the map. He opened it. "There's a resort town that way," he said, nodding right. "It's Bukk-something, *-szehtkereszt*. Back the other way is Lillafured."

"How far?"

"Ten kilometers either way by road. Our friends will have the road covered." He folded the map into his jacket. "I've never had to flush game, but pretty soon I would send someone down that hill to drive us ahead. Wouldn't you?"

"Are there other roads?" Deborah asked.

"None they've bothered to put on the map." He looked around us. "You know, I can't very well walk in this."

"Then you can stay here and interview whoever comes."

His nose came up.

"We'd be grateful," I went on, "if you slow them down, give us a better chance."

"Miserable shit."

We couldn't go fast, and we couldn't go far. Out of rifle range, I hoped; somewhere with a vantage for watching anyone who came down the valley. We stayed in the shadows at the base of the slope, which meant working around clumps of boulders and tangles of brush. On clear ground, our footprints would make a trail easily followed from the ridge.

Peter was breathing heavily after a minute. "You know what they'll do. Yes they'll send down a beater. But they'll also jump somebody ahead in whichever direction we go. We come within fifty yards of where he's set up, he'll perform the executions."

Deborah Wolfe said, "Then we need to get ahead of him, don't we?"

"There are supposed to be caves around here," Peter said.

I didn't want to be trapped in a cave.

"We could hold up in there—"

"For heaven's sake, *walk!*" Deborah's voice, from behind.

Soon, if we didn't want to march into a trap, we had to cut across the valley, hoping they hadn't brought up a rifle by then. If there had been one handy, they would be shooting at us from the ridge by now.

How soon could they post a man ahead? It depended not just on when other help arrived but also on how closely the road followed the rim of the valley. If a team had to go through a mile of woods, we had some time. If the road came within a hundred feet of the rim, not long at all.

I was making assumptions—that they needed manpower or weaponry or both; that they would bother making sure of the kill when exposure would do the job tonight.

So I assumed away and came up with a half hour on the short end, two hours on the long. Either way, time enough to reach the valley's opposite wall. Then what? I was thinking short-term, angling for a few hours, avoiding the reality that a confrontation like had to end in favor of the numbers and guns.

I caught up with Peter. "We'd better get to the other side."

His beard wore a ring of frost. He looked across the meadow. It was no less than a half mile to the trees. After the forest resumed, the land rose again.

"You know," he said, "it might be a good idea to split up. They wouldn't hurt an old man."

"They killed an old woman."

"Obnoxious cow . . . had it coming." His breath was ragged. He slowed, letting Deborah get a few yards ahead, and said, "Regardless of what we do, it's a waste of time, mate. I'm just offering, not insisting—if you take Miss Wolfe, you might stand a small chance."

I couldn't tell whether he was being gallant or lazy. She saw we had fallen behind and screamed, "Can't you two *move*?" We caught up and set off across the meadow.

There were two of them, carrying rifles with telescopic sights. It made spying on them dangerous. They walked about ten yards apart. Both wore short-billed caps, knee-high boots, and shiny black parkas. I had a taste, perhaps, of how a peasant had felt sixty years earlier when the party's enforcers came around to make sure he wasn't digging potatoes for the counterrevolutionaries, or to impose discipline if he was, or to make an example in any case. The distance was almost a mile, and I couldn't make out their faces. One man had a radio in his left hand that he raised to his face. He had given or gotten two reports since they had come into sight.

The other man had a toy that he lifted to his eyes now and then. Once I got an idea what it was, I liked it less than the rifle scopes. It looked like a cross between binoculars and an old Viewmaster but bulkier. The way he turned his head slowly, scanning the hills, he expected to see something. I guessed the something was body heat. I ducked behind my tree each time the device came up and wondered how much energy I radiated past the trunk.

They had stopped now, at the point where we had taken Peter's advice and split up.

One furrow of our tracks ran straight; another angled to the left. The hunters were close enough to the edge of the forest to see that both forks led into the trees. They stopped and consulted, trudged back and forth and examined each trail. I could guess one of the questions they were asking. Was one path a fake, deliberately churned to obscure backtracking? We had shuffled our feet along both routes with no purpose except confusion.

We had had longer than I had expected, more than two hours. The day was well past noon, sundown not much more than four hours away. I had hoped for darkness, but the special binoculars had turned nightfall to the hunters' advantage.

The radio came up, as one of them described the situation. The other man inspected the hillside with his infrared. He was aiming at about my altitude, a hundred or so feet up from the forest floor, but he was focused on the opposite hillside. He was concentrating, lingering at every tree. No tracks veered to that side. His zeroing in told me his estimate of our deviousness; he didn't expect much. That might be his own level of craft, looking for the simplest alternative to the obvious. But I might be underestimating him. He could have jumped back and forth twice in his mind before settling on the south slope.

If he was subtle enough for that, he was capable of trying to deceive an unseen watcher about where his real interest lay. There was no way of knowing, but I made another assumption. Hired guns wouldn't value finesse.

Hired guns weren't expert trackers either. This pair had followed two-hour-old prints across a mountain meadow. But where the trail split, they stood and stared and waited for instructions.

I began to hope.

When the orders came, the two separated. It was the only way to do it. The radio went left, the infrared binoculars went straight ahead. When they reached the first trees five minutes later, I lost sight of the binoculars. The rdio man was nearer, and I saw him from time to time through bare deciduous limbs. He was having no trouble following the tracks. Sunlight had put a shiny crust on the snow, and the path I had taken was as clear as if an army had marched through.

He was out of sight when he followed the tracks around in a large loop. When he found himself dead-ended at a tree, the other side of which bore the trail he had followed five minutes earlier, he stopped and crouched, suspecting that the person who laid the trail might be very close. Minutes passed. He stood up and stared at the bases of trees, especially where the trunks grew close together. He spotted the scraped bark where a leather shoe had slipped. He moved toward it, then began casting in circles. Soon he found the tracks of a man hobbling along on heels or toes deeper into the forest.

That trail showed little attempt at deception. It covered ground, taking advantage of natural features that might throw off pursuit—a hard-frozen stretch of mostly bare earth sheltered by broken trees, a pebbled expanse of ice. But at times the prints were far apart and he could see that his quarry had been running.

He stuck with it for a couple of miles. An open moraine where the snow had melted in patches had no tracks. But somewhere ahead there would be disturbed snow and he would find the trail . . . except it wasn't there to be found. If we had a little luck, he would stalk around the edge of the snow and see places he had crossed as evidence someone had gone before him.

The other man, with the binoculars, would emerge from the trees a hundred yards south and find *his* trail lost in a thicket. The forest rose on, covering hills that swelled into eroded mountains. The hunters might conclude that we had gone on. They wouldn't be able to search every hillside, or every cave.

I had a plan for tonight, but the infrared device made it riskier. There would be forest debris under the snow. If there hadn't been a good melt, some of the rotted stuff might be dry enough to light for a fire.

If they didn't use the infrared on the right hillside, we might get away with it.

The hills were pocked with caves, some substantial according to Peter. The hole we had found, on the south slope, was big enough for one small bear. Three people fitted snugly, eighteen inches out of the weather but quickly drowsy from the excess of carbon dioxide.

I came down the hill one tree at a time.

By half an inch, that was how far he missed my head.

Tree bark exploded. Shards stung my face.

I threw myself down and rolled. No idea whether I was getting into worse trouble, because I didn't know where he was. I came up against the base of a sapling, blinking away grit and tears. Couldn't see a thing useful. Couldn't hear anything except a hammering heart and gaspy breath. A whack like a woodcutter's axe and the sapling's upper several feet folded down. Another slug nipped off a branch. He knew exactly where I was, had a view of the area but couldn't get his trajectory down. I had come over a low hump that obstructed his field. He was on my hillside, significantly distant but not much higher on the slope than I was.

I wanted to run. Foolish primitive urge. I crawled uphill and flattened against the hump. It was part of a stairway of steep ridges, as if pressure had rippled the rocky subsurface.

The shooter could increase his elevation, sharpen the angle to look over obstructions, or he could close in on where he had seen me. He had no reason to think I was armed. But firing from a distance still would appeal to a prudent man who had a choice.

The ripples on the hillside descended gradually, east to west, and I wallowed along mine for twenty feet to a natural depression behind the roots of a tree that had heeled over at about a hundred twenty degrees. If he examined the scene from above, he would take his time before moving. The snow was crushed as far as the sapling he had shot, but no tracks led downhill from there. The trail I had made wiggling along the ridge wouldn't be visible, but if he was patient—if he thought it out and was *certain* I hadn't gotten farther down the slope—he would know in general what I had done. The uncertain part would be whether I had headed east or west while out of sight, and how far.

The radio blast sounded less than a minute later, and seconds after that his footfalls were audible. He hadn't waited at all. He had pushed straight across the slope to make the kill. At the radio's next burst, he halted. I could hear his voice, the words unintelligible. Bringing someone up to date, could be a base command or another team beating the brush. His partner would have heard the shots but was out of contact; they had shared a radio. Between snow-covered roots I could see him, fifty feet away. The rifle was braced against his right hip, muzzle pointed at the last place he had seen me. The radio was a few inches from his left ear. He was concentrating on the area near the sapling but cast nervous glances in all directions. The face was square and dark, with sharp features, fixed in businesslike concentration. He said something, then pushed the radio receiver into a pocket.

He lifted the rifle to his shoulder and aimed. The angle was too shallow to let him see much of the ground near the sapling. He searched the area through the scope.

Then he decided to come down for a closer look. I had gone straight over the hump, then lay against the tree where he had nearly got me. If he took that course, it would block part of his view of what lay past the tree. He wanted to approach at an angle, and he didn't want to slide on his bottom. He lowered the rifle to present arms and looked for an easy route. The nearest option was to his left, which would take him away from me. He paced off about twenty feet, took a sighting with the scope. There was something about it he didn't like, perhaps the thickness of the brush between him and the sapling. He rejected that route and came back.

He saw me when he was just the other side of the root tangle, swung the rifle down. Slugs tore through wood or earth, cut a numbing streak down my back. I was lunging when he fired but couldn't reach his feet. He backed away and jerked the muzzle lower and it struck a root and bounced, and the next three shots went high and I got my hands around his legs, intent on pulling myself up under the line of fire, but I was halfway out of the roots when his knees buckled and he came down onto my back.

There were glimmers of polished wood stock down among the roots. He was trying to crawl down there. His cap was gone and the sandy hair was stiff. I went after him. A left-handed rabbit punch had no effect. In a moment his fingers were going to touch the rifle stock. I pulled his radio from the snow and swung it down twice, and the second time it came apart in my hand.

Now both men were out of touch with the base.

I stripped off his parka and rolled him through the snow. Fixed it up quickly so he was slumped against the decapitated tree, wrists belted behind the trunk, bootlaces holding a handkerchief gag. My coat went over his head. If you didn't look too closely, he could be a fugitive taking a rest.

I settled down at the base of a tree, warm in the quilted parka, hat bill low on my forehead, and used the man's rifle to take a bead on the lower slope. The man with the binoculars was too intelligent to call out. He had heard gunfire, too many shots, and he was taking no chances. I didn't see him approach. The sun had climbed away, putting the north slope in shadow. The trees and thickets lost their firm edges. Thirty minutes after I took cover, the shape wearing my coat shook violently and bounced against the sapling to a rhythm of staccato snaps—four or five, I lost track—and sagged forward.

I lay motionless.

His approach took another half hour. He came across the hillside. There was no need to make sure of the kill, but something about it bothered him. In the gray afternoon the message of the slumped figure wasn't clear. He was fifty feet from the body when his posture changed. He straightened and then froze, seeming to anticipate the next event. For more than a minute I had had the crosshairs centered on his chest.

24

"Can you see anything?"

"No."

"Do you know how to operate the bloody thing?"

"No."

"Then you can't expect to see anything." Peter Rice lay on his elbows a few feet from me, chin on the back of his hands.

I shifted my weight, trying to ease the discomfort of my back. Wolfe had said the furrow the bullet had made wasn't more than an inch long: I should stop complaining, focus on business. I pressed the night-viewer against my face. The images were indecipherable, puddles of warmth radiating in a night of frozen black. One puddle was the engine compartment of a car. A hot ghost had walked down the road to relieve someone posted on the crest, and after a less radiant shape came up the road five minutes later, the car was the only warm object. Spots on the lodge itself glowed faintly. Windows on the ground floor shimmered like curtains. The stone walls were only beginning to leak heat.

"I'd say they invited themselves in," Peter said.

I hoped the owners hadn't been present. "Ask him again how many."

He spoke softly to the man beside him. The light from the building was practically useless, but it highlighted the barrel of the pistol Peter held against the man's head. Our prisoner was gagged, but he could grunt and squeal. He had been difficult all the way through the forest. My not having shot him seemed more and more a bad decision. He had dropped the rifle and raised his hands so fast that a moment passed before I remembered he was a hired killer who had blown apart his teammate and I should shoot him. By then I couldn't. He knew when to cry uncle. Now Peter Rice wore the man's quilted black coat and the pistol he had carried under it, and if our friend, who said his name was Georgy, stood up and started screaming for help I didn't suppose Peter would shoot. Georgy already had my measure. It hadn't taken him a minute to size up the two reporters. Once he decided none of us would shoot, or crush a testicle when a question went unanswered, he turned smirkingly unhelpful.

I heard a snort and a couple of strangled sounds.

"He says there are more than enough of them to kill us," Peter reported.

I went back to the viewer. If they had a guard on this side, he was well hidden. Otherwise I didn't need to repeat the count. Four vehicles, including a minivan and a white sedan. Eight to twelve men in the lodge, settling in for the night. At least two other vehicles and four or five agents scouring the roads. A couple of lookouts patrolling on foot. The team that had gone out when Georgy and his friend went silent had retreated an hour after full dark. We had watched them from the south slope, four men coming across the meadow, four going back. No sharpshooter left in a tree.

Deborah Wolfe crept up beside me. "A car would be nice," she said. Her teeth rattled and her body trembled. Signs of hypothermia. She had done half the complaining of Peter and me. *Not that cold*, she'd insisted. I tried to forget that she and her pal Kajdi had started this ball rolling. If we hadn't gone to Baja, several people might still be alive. Kajdi, arguably József's men, the Holts, Józsefne . . . and if she ever got her story on the air it would still feature right-wing commandoes plotting a coup.

"A car would be very nice," I agreed.

"Could you start one?"

"Yes."

"So what—" her teeth clicked "—what's holding you up?"

"Patrick is reluctant to be shot at again," Peter said. "If someone inside doesn't expect to hear a car starting, they'll come investigate."

"Put your cap on," I said. "There's another way of doing it."

He put on the short-billed cap he had taken from Georgy.

The last car setting out on patrol had headed north. Fifteen minutes before that, an Opel with two men aboard had driven south. We left Georgy and the pistol with Deborah and crept a quarter mile down the road. If they returned this way, they would be driving uphill on frozen ruts. It took forty minutes.

Approached from behind, wearing our black parkas and short-billed caps, carrying our rifles and other gear, we looked like friends. The Opel slowed, tires spinning. The driver didn't want to stop on the hill, but the fact we were out here at all meant something was going on. The heavier man walking on the right kept raising his rifle at an invisible target in the woods. The brake lights flashed on. The driver cranked down the window, and I put a gun barrel in his face. I pointed the flashlight at his hands. Peter's light blazed through the opposite window. He barked a command, and the passenger opened his door. I flicked the light at the driver. He understood well enough, tried to slip the car into gear and the wheels spun and whined. I backed up two steps, leveled the rifle and aimed carefully.

He stopped the engine and climbed out.

Peter herded his man around front. Using one man's belt, he cinched the two together, a left wrist to a right wrist, as if they were holding hands. When he patted them down from behind, he got two automatics.

I went back up the road on foot. There seemed to be more lights on in the lodge but no sign of alarm. I walked past. Deborah crouched as far as possible from her prisoner, pistol in both hands. The gun swung wildly. She gave a yelp. "Patrick?"

"Quit pointing it at me. And be quiet."

"Are we ready?"

"What happened here?"

"I was so cold. . . . He knocked the gun out of my hand, kicked it away."

"But you got it back."

"I was so angry!"

I couldn't read Georgy's expression in the dark, thought about rearranging it with the rifle butt, just to be sure. I got him on his feet, shoved him onto the road. Halfway past the lodge he made his dash: threw a shoulder into the woman, then raced across the snow. I caught up and tripped him with the rifle, and he made a lot of noise going down. I crouched, held my breath and waited for the front door to open. It would have been much easier to leave a body at the roadside. That was the threat I whispered, and I think he understood: I would take the easy way.

Peter had reversed the Opel and had his two prisoners standing in the headlights. He added Georgy and forced them to walk ahead of the car. It was mostly downhill for a mile. We picked up speed toward the bottom and Peter swung out and passed them. They had no guns and no radios. He looked at me and said, "Personally, I would feel better if they were under a snow bank."

I thought of József Cseve and his co-conspirators, woefully inadequate. Finding it not too hard to kill separated the survivors from the also-rans.

I looked over the seat back. "Are you thawing?"

She nodded. Feet up on the seat, arms around her knees, holding in whatever warmth remained. "Peter's right. We'd be better off if they couldn't talk."

I read Peter's map by flashlight. Forty-five kilometers or so to a highway numbered 25, by which point we would be coming out of the hills, then south twenty kilometers to a main road and then ninety minutes to Budapest.

He read my mind. "Your choice. We won't be any better off in Buda. We *might* make it to a border."

I folded the map. My fingers had been numb for hours. Feeling was coming back all at once, burning needles. I watched the road. A fork would give us the illusion of choice. The icy furrows ran straight across meadows, and crooked down mountains, but there was no secondary branch promising a better bet than the main one. I disliked the inevitability; wondered what sort of idiot drives to his execution just because that's where the road leads.

We had all kinds of choices. We could pull off the road for a nap in the snow. . . .

I realized I had been drifting, almost asleep. I thought I should keep an eye on the road, keep Peter company. The headlights showed a three-sided tunnel of white, stark black above the white, vibrating and sashaying, hypnotic really.

I shook myself awake. "Do you want me to spell you?"

"You'd run us off the road."

I settled back. Closed my eyes; he was doing all right, holding the car at the center of the trough, keeping the speed below forty; I closed my eyes and opened them with a start an indefinite time later, but there was no reason for the start. We were on flat terrain, the only headlights our own. I looked at my watch. Fifty minutes since we had left the men. It wasn't long enough for pursuit to be close behind. Trudging uphill to the lodge would have taken them twenty-five minutes—at least. If a chase car had gotten on the road immediately, it would have had to cover the same ground we had in half the time. Peter had been averaging thirty-five, say, which meant pursuit would have to average seventy, and there was no way they could do it on this road.

Twenty minutes from now the situation would be different. They would only need to have covered the same distance in not quite two-thirds the time. An aggressive driver in a heavy car wouldn't find that impossible. I looked behind us. No lights.

Sometime in the next twenty minutes that would change. They would overtake us, and it would happen five or ten kilometers from the junction with the bigger road. No doubt about the rest of it.

"Could you drive a little faster?"

We were bouncing and weaving at thirty k.p.h. But he could go faster, if he wanted to, and I wondered why he didn't want to.

He spoke to Deborah Wolfe. "Bugger wakes up from his nap, all warm and comfy, and complains 'e ain't bein' driven right."

He was making *plausible* time. The way the light car wiggled in the ruts, the passengers would think it was good time. Not good enough, as it would turn out, but we needn't know that until something came up behind and slammed us off the road.

I let the thought develop. We had been tagged all the way to Miskolc. It could have been Peter. He had called Wolfe, and he could have made another call—not to the security forces but to the Europa Foundation. A free-lance journalist could use a democracy-building grant now and then to tide him over. But Peter had accepted that Innes had been somebody's mole and he had taken the argument a step further: If Innes, why not Gabor? But why shouldn't he, if it wouldn't matter in the end. We had been heading south then, into the forest, where Peter's friends could lay their next trap. It would be the backup plan. If the ambush at the hotel didn't work, we would drive down into the mountains. *Try not to kill the girl,* he might have said. *I'll fill her head with a colorful story about the CIA.*

I sat and picked at that version and liked it. He hadn't been much help, slowed us down when we had to get to cover. If we wanted to run off into the woods, Peter would just stay behind and wait to be shot.

Right.

He had helped hijack the Opel, true, but I'd had a rifle then. He hadn't shot me in the back when he was guarding Georgy with the pistol. But that proved nothing. He had never had a no-risk opportunity. Possibly not the stomach. If he had put a bullet behind my ear, he would have had to kill Wolfe as well. He liked her. He wasn't a monster. Just a free-lancer on the other side.

That was one version. I was never supposed to have made it to the second rendezvous. István and company were supposed to have taken care of all of us at the hotel.

I tried a different spin. Peter Rice had made one call. Deborah Wolfe had made the other. She was cozy with Andras Kajdi, chomping to expose the fascist putsch, rebelling against Daddy's history lessons, perhaps. That could fit, but other facts didn't. She had driven like hell at the lodge. Kicked ass when Peter wanted to call it quits. Held Georgy when she could have sent him to alert his friends.

Or—the possibility I had settled for until now—the Holts or I had been under surveillance from the start. I had met Glasgow and her boys on my home turf, the hotel. That had been stupid. It wouldn't have been hard to tag any of us from the Corvinus to Dolce Vita and the train station.

Peter spoke softly. "You figure they'll be on us soon."

I didn't answer.

"I don't want to land this little tin can in a ditch. But if the big sedan comes after us, we'll have a problem."

"It's possible."

"Could've been avoided, you know."

"If you'd driven faster?"

"If we'd shot three men. You were never in the army, I can tell. Too squeamish when it comes to improving the odds. You wouldn't leave a fat old man by himself to freeze. Couldn't bring yourself to pop Georgy and the others."

"I didn't hear you proposing it."

"I thought about it. How long do we have, do you think?"

"If they're coming, ten minutes."

"We should be looking for a place to stop."

"Stop?"

"Improve the odds for the rest of the night."

The thought of being alone with him in the dark with a gun froze my bones, but he was right.

We went around a shallow bend a mile later, sliding left and bouncing off the plowed-up fender and I said, "All right. Here."

Peter stopped us a hundred feet from where the turn straightened. "Deborah, love, it's your turn to drive."

She saw us take the rifles and didn't protest. Just put the car in gear, moved off.

We climbed the right embankment. It felt like clear country behind us, ice-coated meadows and not many hills or trees to block the stars. The Opel's taillights disappeared. We settled in, quilted bellies on the snow. I had kept Peter in front of me. But soon enough—if a car appeared—I would have my attention full of other things. Right now it was almost full of stars, which spilled overhead from the elevated northeast horizon all the way west to the upturned soles of my feet. Celestial trash, like sequins on Ida's dress.

"Should we have told her to wait ahead?"

"The most likely outcome," Peter said, "is we're going to bloody fucking freeze to death. She'll wait. Have you ever gone gunning?"

He meant hunting. I said, "No."

"Take a hare. You lop off the head, dispose of the viscera, there's so damn little left to the thing, meat, tendon, bone, seems unlikely it could ever have been anything."

I could feel my own viscera trembling. I was too cold to talk.

"If you'd gone to medical college," Peter said, "you would understand that that's all there is in the car behind us: meat, tendon, bone."

I let him talk.

"It helps to get in the right frame of mind," Peter said.

After that he shut up, but only for a minute because then we saw headlights. More than a mile down the road, coming fast. That was the key. János the farmer or plumber wouldn't be slamming down this narrow dark road. This was somebody in a hurry. I aimed the rifle a few feet above the road and a few feet in front of the bend.

"I've done it before, you see," Peter said. "For instance, that little shit Sipos."

I looked but couldn't really see him.

"Thought he was going to do you for his bosses and it didn't seem fair."

"You're not a journalist, are you?"

"I most certainly am. Ask my chum Jacob."

Half mile, closing.

Quarter mile, hell bent.

Hell-bent indeed.

I put my eye to the scope.

I couldn't tell where the first shots hit.

Then the burst tank lit up the sky. The back wheels lifted and the sedan flipped forward and sledded down the road on its roof, hit a shoulder obstruction and flipped again. Slammed an embankment. Spun its tail into the middle of the roadway. It stopped there, a hundred yards past us. Without windshield or windows, I'd seen them go, without front tires or headlights, without anything visible inside except raging incandescence, and no one trying to get out.

25

"*You've been ordered* out of the country," Magdalena Glasgow said.

I didn't bother to answer. It was her office, her speech.

"You don't respect the local government's commitment to democratic values."

I did, actually, and I was grateful that the embassy had had me on ice for sixteen hours. "What about the others?"

"Miss Wolfe reached Vienna this afternoon. The Englishman landed in Prague ninety minutes ago. They're out of danger." Magdalena Glasgow spread her hands. What was my problem?

"They may not be out of danger from the Europa Foundation."

"Mr. McCarry, I would forget those slanders."

"They're not slanders."

"When you lack proof, what's left is slander. You were set upon by bandits. They were not affiliated with Mr. Gabor's foundation."

"No more than Innes was."

The sour face gave away nothing. She knew the score, but singing to it didn't fit the diplomatic program.

"Innes must have been in the government's pocket for a long time," I said. "Operating all those years without Tamás Gabor noticing."

It would sink in, or not. Anything she believed about Innes, she could believe about Gabor.

"You might find it interesting," she said, "that Mr. Gabor was on television this morning urging the government to deal severely with terrorists."

"Terrorists."

"The fascists, who were plotting terrorist acts. The security forces raided a small opposition party's office last night. They found weapons." Behind her head, a scallop of dirty ice held the window snug to the frame, keeping the inside air stale.

Jeremy Butts opened the door. "Sorry to interrupt. We ought to get going."

In the hall, Butts said, "The lady's really pissed. Good thing you didn't rile her. She liked Sampson, trained him herself."

We picked up Carl downstairs. "Did you make your fortune in Budapest?" Carl asked.

I didn't want to talk to them.

"He's still sore over the needle," Jeremy said.

We rode the rest of the way in silence. They came with me into the terminal, walked me past two goons in black topcoats and out to the plane. Four hours later I was in London.

A week after that I was in the south of France.

The young radio reporter crossed the Metropole's terrace, determination in every step. The wind tugged at her wool skirt and pushed short brown hair across her forehead. Rain spattered the steps to the terrace. Most of the yachts had abandoned the harbor. There was a clear sweep of choppy gray sea nibbling at the beach. Winter on the Riviera put ice in the bones, unless you had come from somewhere colder.

It had taken us five days to get in touch. We needed, she said, to get things straight.

We went into the bar. Wolfe dropped the *International Herald-Tribune* on the table, told the waiter two brandies and coffee. "I've got a couple weeks' vacation," she said. "NPR wouldn't put what I came up with on the air, but they don't want me to resign. So I'm taking time. That's what they say, taking time."

"Have you talked to Peter Rice?"

"No . . . he's hard to find sometimes."

She drank her brandy quickly when it came.

I glanced at the folded newspaper and understood why. And wondered if I had needed to tell Magdalena Glasgow anything, or if she had got there herself. The car-bombing in London dominated the front page. There were proper expressions of horror from all quarters. Promises to root out terrorism whatever its source. Hagiographies of the international financier who had been the bombing's principal victim. Paragraphs about his philanthropy.

With or without my help, Glasgow had decided that Tamás Gabor owed her for the agent she had trained.

Jeremy or Carl, or one of her other eager pups, had delivered her regrets.

Photo: Julia Ferguson

About the Author

James L. Ross knows the Wall Street scene first-hand. A former journalist, he is the author under several names of short stories and novels, including 2011's *Long Pig*. A new story, "Bears in Mind," appeared in *Alfred Hitchcock's Mystery Magazine* in January 2012.

If you enjoyed this book, look for these other titles
published by PERFECT CRIME BOOKS.

LONG PIG James L. Ross
318 pages. $15.95. ISBN: 978-1-935797-10-4

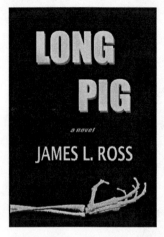

QUARRY Max Allan Collins
234 pages. $14.95. ISBN: 9781-935797-01-2

LAST ISLAND SOUTH John C. Boland
246 pages. $12.95. ISBN: 978-0-9825157-8-5

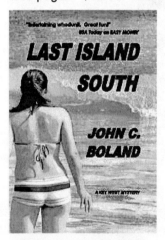

PRESENCE OF MIND Edward Cline
196 pages. $14.95. ISBN: 978-0-9825157-0-9

Available at bookstores, Amazon, and at www.PerfectCrimeBooks.com